I WISH YOU WERE NOT HERE

DEEPSHIKHA SAW

Inkfeathers Publishing
www.inkfeathers.com

I Wish You Were Not Here
by Deepshikha Saw
Paperback Edition

First Published in India in 2022
by Inkfeathers Publishing, New Delhi 110095

Copyright © Deepshikha Saw 2022
Cover Illustrations by Shivani Gautam Sinha
Interior Illustrations by Arjita Dangwal

All rights reserved.
ISBN 9789390882311

www.inkfeathers.com

CONTENTS

PROLOGUE

It was the first day of the year 2022. Shivangi sat in her room under a blanket as the Delhi winters made her shiver. The cloudy weather was beautiful with no sign of sun anywhere. Those were the last few days of her winter vacation, as her online classes were going to start again.

She opened her new diary and filled out the first page. She had been writing a diary for a few years. As the pandemic hit the world, she became more passionate about writing about her own life. Before beginning the first entry, she remembered her last year's diary and decided to go through it. She randomly opened a page, and it landed on an entry of 15th June 2021. It was about her conversation with her elder sister Nitya.

It was one of the entries where rather than writing as Shivangi, she had written the diary from her sister's perspective.

"I stared outside the window. I had everything I needed during the quarantine except the freedom to be out there, no matter even if in a mask!"

Shivangi was reminded of the day of that conversation. Nitya had tested positive for Covid, and after her recovery, she had shared her experience with Shivangi. Through the last two years, that was the conversation that had always left her with tears. Shivangi was a bit hesitant to continue as she didn't want to start her new year with tears or memories of the past.

Maybe the universe wants me to remember that even if it's a new beginning, I should not forget the past we carry, Shivangi thought as she continued reading.

"That one month of isolation helped me reflect on my thoughts and my life. I am sure, just like me, thousands of others would have felt the same. The troubling silence when you look outside the window. You see people in masks or a car passing while you are in your room, having that last slice of pizza that you ordered for yourself on the weekend. But you cannot enjoy the food when you are sick. A lot of people had lost their taste buds, and for a long time, I was lucky enough to still enjoy my favourite food, but soon, my taste bud had gone. I was feeling the desperate need to taste something, but there was nothing I could do about it."

She remembered how Nitya had been staying alone in a room when she had to quarantine herself. She was away from her family, living in altogether a different city.

"There was a time when I was tired of watching all the Netflix shows, movies, and even the cringiest YouTube videos. They did keep me entertained, but then I needed to feel fresh air touching me and bringing the ultimate joy. Like when you are watching a movie that beautifully describes nature while you are caged within the four walls, the craving to go out increases.

I still remember the time when I was working out at home. I noticed a headache originating behind my eyes. Soon, I felt dizziness and difficulty in breathing. I knew the symptoms, but I couldn't believe what was happening; or let's say, I didn't want to believe it."

It was the last sentence on that page. Shivangi knew what was written on the next page, and she grew more hesitant, but with shivering hands, she turned to the next page.

"One morning, I could feel it all. I knew for the last three days that

I was sick, but I waved it off, considering it to be a normal fever. I was damn sure it would go away, but sometimes, as they say, too much confidence can be too bad. I was shocked when I saw my results were positive. The loss of smell and taste took a toll on me. Being a foodie, I felt like my soul had been sucked out of me. I was so devastated. It was not fair, but I am here, talking about it, which proves that I am a fighter. Even though somewhere I knew, it was tough to digest that I could pass such a dangerous phase, especially for my parents."

"Of course, you are a fighter," Shivangi remembered telling her that.

"That feeling of weakness, which I no longer feel, still makes me feel dejected. The duration of one month to recover was too much for me. The irony is, after fourteen days of quarantine, I was sure I would be tested negative. I had already packed my bags to go home. But when I got tested again, I was disappointed. It was still positive. For the first fourteen days, even if I wasn't feeling well, there was optimism, but when it happened again, I lost all hope. Those fourteen days felt like four years to me. It felt like I had visited hell!

I could not sleep at night. The reality I was living in felt more like a nightmare. I could barely walk to the kitchen, but I still had to cook. I preferred making rice as it was easier. I had to keep the surroundings clean, do those household chores, and not forget to make healthy food and drinks for my immunity. That time I realised how the absence of my mother had affected me badly. Yet, I somehow managed, so I do feel proud of myself.

Handling the situation all alone, cooking, and managing on my own was no less than a life exam. It was like the gods were testing me. Not only for me, but it was a life exam for everyone who tested positive. The creator of the universe wanted to know if we creatures are worthy of being a part of his creation.

That phase didn't go easily. Even after recovery, I had a bad cough, and the feeling of weakness didn't fade away. It has been long since I recovered, but the presence of the virus is still alive in me. It had become a part of me. It feels like I was someone else, and now that part of me has gone but it still keeps visiting me. That one month of loneliness took the worst out of me. I can't believe the hardest time of my life has passed. I, obviously, haven't proved anything, but it has made me a little wiser.

I understand that things will never be the same again, it is obvious, but I realise it now. Situations like these can bring the worst and the best out of us human beings. Adapting is the only option for survival, and we humans are capable of anything. We are even capable of forgetting this pandemic once it is over."

Shivangi recalled everything her sister had said. As she had expected, her eyes were welled up with tears. She closed her old diary and opened her new one. In the first entry, she wrote, "Dear Diary. Happy New Year. I want to tell you so much already, but let me start by saying, Thank you."

Shivangi felt thankful for the journey of the last two years. Even though filled with challenges, they have helped her grow so much.

"I am extremely grateful for this life," she wrote in big block letters and with that closed her diary. She then slipped under her blanket in the gripping cold of January.

CHOCOLATE AND CANDIES

"We don't know when this will end, Diuja. I miss those times when everything was normal."

It was, as usual, a hot day in May. Being the most talkative one, Shivangi couldn't stop ranting about the current situation.

"I remember the time when we all used to hang out together. We could go anywhere in the world. We only needed money to travel, and now even if we have money, we don't have the freedom. Anyhow, being happy at the moment is helpful for now."

"I know, bro. Those were the times of fun. After all, we had a normal life," replied Diuja frowning.

"Don't worry, guys. Everything will be fine soon. We have to hang in there," said Samaira, the most optimistic one in the group.

"What if things don't go back to normal? What if we are stuck? All the countries are fighting this pandemic, and yet I haven't heard any good news of overcoming it anytime soon," said Shivangi taking a bite of the last chocolate left in the refrigerator. "I don't want to spend my birthday like this amidst a pandemic and in lockdown. It really sucks," she cried again.

"We have to stick to what it is, guys. The whole world is suffering. It's not only us. In fact, we don't even have any problems as compared to so many other people," again, Samaira had to explain to her closest friends. She was reading one of the bestsellers and had learned to be positive no matter what. Well, good books can certainly change lives.

"You are right, Samu. We should be more grateful that we are alive, and our loved ones are safe. The pain people are facing around the globe is indescribable, and I will be writing about what we are going through," said Shivangi with confidence and passion in her eyes.

"Yes, definitely, go for it!" said Diuja while working on her new illustration for her art collection.

"Do you guys remember the time when we used to hang out at my house? Our mom's chit-chatting as usual, as we had our favourite shakes," Samaira said in enthusiasm, remembering that time.

"I so miss those times. And now we will have to make Dalgona coffee at home," laughed Shivangi.

Diuja felt left out as she lived in another city. They haven't met each other for years.

"Do you guys remember our trip to Delhi? We all had the most famous *paratha* at *Chandni Chowk*. Shopping at *Sarojini*. We brought so much stuff that we had to buy another bag to carry the things," Diuja said as all three of them burst out laughing. "We had so much fun watching movies, eating at the restaurant, and exploring the city. When will those days come back? I am tired of cleaning utensils and sweeping the house while dreaming of our Goa trip."

"Oh yes, Goa trip! It is still on our bucket list. And don't remind me of Delhi, I miss its food and shopping. I can't imagine my life without it," Shivangi whined as she licked her chocolate-coated fingers.

Both Diuja and Shivangi sighed.

"For now, we can simply imagine and not step out of our homes. It's the best option," Samaira sounded dominating.

"How are you so fine with the situation? Are you not sad that we can't hang out anymore?" asked Shivangi in curiosity.

Well, Samaira is an introvert and anti-social. She enjoys her own company. Sometimes being weird and clingy is her most challenging trait, which only her friends can handle.

"Shivangi, you know the answer. Anyways I am enjoying being at home. Besides, I have books to read, shows to watch, and Pulu to play with," Samaira said lazily.

Samaira is so lazy to meet her friends, or for that matter, anyone who is a human. She strives to enjoy her own company. Pulu, her cat, is her only comfort zone. She talks to her, feeds her, and communicates with her in her mother tongue Bengali. The mesmerizing eyes of Pulu are enough for her to melt. Even Pulu reciprocates back the love.

"Samaira seems happy. We both are the only ones missing our social gatherings," Diuja mumbled.

"Yeah, but we will be fine. After all, we have to do other things too. You focus on your art, and I will focus on my writing," said Shivangi with a smile.

Shivangi couldn't forget those times with all the fun she had with her friends and family. Now she was stuck in a single place. Having video calls all day and missing the touch of meeting people and social gatherings.

While Diuja missed the famous *pani puri* of Lucknow, Samaira missed her hostel. She couldn't wait for her college to start. Being a medical student, she knew the colleges would open early, even if the pandemic didn't end.

The group drowned themselves in the memories of the good times. They thought about the times when the excitement of going to the theatres kept them on their toes. They would always rush to buy the ticket for the first show, which was incomplete without the cheese flavoured popcorn in one hand and cold drinks in the other.

"Do you remember how frustrating it was to pass through crowds in parties and bookstores? And the roads filled with traffic," said Shivangi. She remembered how she had once seen young children selling balloons, and her eyes had welled up. Out of sympathy, she bought the balloon, and the smile that radiated on the child's face made her heart swell.

"Of course. But even then, it was still fun," added Diuja.

"I remember jogging early in the morning. People would bring their pets for a walk. And when I would return, there were gathering of the aunties in the society and the children playing together. There was so much noise and light in the streets, right?"

"Now all we see are masks, and the smell of a sanitiser is the most prevalent thing we can come across for now," Diuja said, as she wasn't a morning person.

"You guys remember how everything started to change after we heard about the virus spreading in the world? We all were taking it so lightly at first when we watched the news of the outbreak. Even the social media was all about this new virus," Samaira said.

"Yeah, it was January when the first case was detected in Kerala," Shivangi added.

"Yes. Also, Shivangi, do you remember? We were at your home chatting when the lockdown was announced on the news," Samaira said.

***

March 24, 2020

Samaira had come home from her hostel a few days ago. The Covid outrage was spreading in India, and many schools and colleges had already been closed. Samaira's medical college was one of them. Shivangi was eagerly waiting for her childhood friend cum neighbour. The last time they met was a year ago when Samaira left for the hostel. When Samaira reached home, Shivangi was standing outside her house. The moment they saw each other, their faces lit up. They waved from afar, as Samaira had travelled amidst this outbreak, and they needed to be safe.

Later that day, she freshened up and visited Shivangi's house. She greeted Shivangi's parents, Mr. Sanjay and Mrs. Amita, her grandma, and her younger brother Ayaansh, who had completed his twelfth, but the date for the exam was postponed. Both Shivangi and Samaira sat in the veranda to catch up on their talks. Samaira talked about her hostel life and unknowingly spilled about the bad habits she had adopted, like smoking and drinking.

"You know they are bad for health. I can understand you got the habit, but you need to have control," Shivangi said as Samaira told her stories about partying and having drinks. Samaira waved it away a few times, but when Shivangi kept pestering her, she nodded and agreed that she would try to cut it down. Shivangi was satisfied and finally dropped the topic. They then ended up talking till dinner time.

***

They were enjoying these leisure days. Sometimes they would video call Diuja and would gossip for hours. They even did the task for 22nd March together. The nation was asked to perform a task to express gratitude towards all the Covid warriors.

"On Sunday at exactly 5 pm, we all stand at the doors, balconies, windows of our homes, and give them all a 5-minute standing ovation. We clap our hands, beat our plates, and ring our bells to boost their morale, salute their service."

They had so much fun, and Shivangi was stunned to see so much unity. At every house, every person was standing, showing their support.

***

Today the prime minister was going to address the nation again. Samaira's family had joined Shivangi's family at their home. It was going to be 8 pm. The news channel was on mute. The adults discussed what new steps would be taken while the youngsters were having fun talking about any new task they may have to do.

"It has started. Unmute the channel, Ayaansh," Amita said.

The prime minister started by praising everyone for their effort in the Sunday task, and Ayaansh beamed with pride, at which Shivangi and Samaira giggled. They expected the next few sentences to be about another task, but what came next shocked everyone and changed their lives.

"From midnight tonight onwards, the entire country, please listen carefully, the entire country shall go under complete lockdown."

The silence was now filled with questions and worries. What is a lockdown? We can't go out for 21 days! How will we buy groceries? What about our jobs?

Samaira's family bid a fast bye to Shivangi's family and left. The men now had to go and buy groceries to stock for the whole three weeks. And the nation was in chaos.

***

Present

"Of course. Omg, how can I forget? We were stupidly waiting for the next task, and a whole mission got assigned to us," Shivangi said.

"And now 21 days have changed to almost two months, and we have no idea if this will be extended too," Diuja said.

"Okay, guys. Don't worry too much. Just take care of yourselves and stay safe," Samaira said. "I have to go now."

"Yes, even I have to go and work on my art, and Shivangi also has to go write. So, we'll talk later," Diuja said.

They bid goodbye and cut the call. Shivangi sat there and thought about all this.

All of a sudden, everything had stopped. Schools and colleges were closed. Even the studies turned into online classes. She was nostalgic, thinking about the moments before the pandemic. She was confused at her thoughts. On the one hand, she wanted to go out, and at the same time, she was thankful to be alive and safe at her house.

Shaking off the thoughts, she wandered out to the hall where her father was eating mangoes. "Papa, I know how much you love mangoes, but you have been eating it since morning. Even after lunch, you haven't stopped eating," Shivangi said.

"This is the mango season *beta* (dear). It comes once a year. How can I not enjoy this time? Also, I am thankful to enjoy this privilege of eating mangoes during the time of this pandemic."

"Well, that's true, Papa. We are privileged to enjoy all these, while the pandemic has affected a lot of people drastically. Losing loved ones is the worst kind of pain, and a lot of people in the world are grieving for their loss."

"This is a sad time for us. So being thankful for whatever life has given us is the least we can do to stay happy and positive at the moment. If we spread positivity during these tough times when everything is filled with negativity, then we are spreading hope to the world," her father said as he took another mango from the basket.

"But Papa, how am I supposed to be happy when I know people are suffering out there. Even we lost a family member. Being happy during these times feels wrong to me."

"*Beta*, you don't always have to feel that way. When you feel good, you shouldn't stop yourself. Losing my uncle has been a huge loss for us. Even after 20 days of hospitalization, they couldn't save him. I have lost my mentor, who always helped me. Losing the people close to me makes me sad. I certainly feel like breaking down, but I know at the same time, today we are alive. We don't know about the future, so we should live our best and enjoy every moment."

The pandemic helped Sanjay to focus more on the privilege he had even when he was broken from inside. He chose to be happy and alive at the moment rather than being sad about the incidents happening around him.

"Yes, Papa, you are right. There is a quote I heard in a movie, 'Yesterday is history, tomorrow is a mystery, but today is a gift. That is why it is called the present.' And today, I can feel it."

***

Some realization never comes easily. It might take a pandemic for some to realise the importance of the minor things in their lives. Shivangi was sitting one day, eating the dark chocolate her dad had brought after she kept demanding for days.

During the lockdown, Sanjay had to go to office as he worked at the Airport. He had duties to fulfil during this time of the pandemic. Being a stubborn daughter, she had asked for some chocolates, and he could never deny her. He happily brought it one day, which made her smile. Today, she realised how privileged she was. She can ask for chocolates during such a time. Her privilege allows her to have all the other luxuries, where people struggle for basic food.

She wondered if she should feel sad about it. Of course, somewhere, she had the guilt of having chocolates, sitting at home binge-watching shows, having fun with her brother while people outside were fighting this virus. Somehow just sitting at her home, having that luxury, and not being able to help others was affecting her thoughts. So, she went to her mom with this feeling.

"Mummy, I need to tell you something," she started softly.

"Go ahead, *beta*," her mother asked curiously. Shivangi's mom, Amita, was someone who loved to work. Even during the pandemic with no maid to help in the house, she never complained. She does sometimes ask her kids to help with chores. The only time she relaxes is in the afternoon when she watches the latest news and takes a sound nap.

"I feel bad about what is happening outside. I am eating chocolates, watching shows, working out and whatnot while laborers, unemployed people, medical staff, police officers, and others are suffering and fighting this virus. I am at peace, having this piece of chocolate that papa brought, even he needs to step out of the house. And I am not contributing anything? Am I being selfish during such times of crisis? Or is my conscience dying?"

Her mom smiled, gently pulled her towards herself, and kept her hand on her head.

"Having these thoughts are natural, *beta*. I know people are suffering, and you are concerned about them. But what else can you do? You are still a student. You are already helping the healthcare workers by staying at home. Coming to you enjoying your luxury, you were born with it. Yes, you shouldn't demand chocolates during these times, but yet again, taking care of yourself and your mental health is equally important. If you are not happy, how can you expect others around you to be? So, you are not being selfish by taking care of yourself," she explained calmly. "Yes, there are people out in the world fighting every day for food, while we have it easy. It is a privilege *beta*, and we should be grateful for it. That is what we can do for now. Besides, it is important to do things for yourself too. Just be thankful for the life you have."

Shivangi felt lighter after her conversation with her mom. She smiled at her, hugged her, and left the room for her mother to have her afternoon nap.

But these things still bothered her somewhere. She could not deny what was going on in the world. She passed the rest of her day as usual, in the room with the AC temperature set at 25 degrees Celsius, scrolling through Instagram. She was having a good time with herself when Ayaansh decided to annoy her. And as usual, they both ended up arguing about who was more productive during the lockdown.

Shivangi couldn't stop thinking about how privileged she was. She decided to talk about this with Ayaansh, who was busy wasting time on his phone.

"Bro, don't you think that we shouldn't complain about our lives anymore? I mean, some part of us used to do that earlier. The appreciation of life was never our priority, but now we all are in a much better space. Considering how life has taught us to appreciate even the smallest gestures."

Ayaansh kept staring at his phone, trying to act ignorant of her elder sister. But what she said got him thinking, and he couldn't pretend much.

"*Di* (elder sister), this reminds me of the word 'privilege.' What comes to our mind after thinking of that word? Money, luxury, happiness, opportunities, and what else?" he asked, trying to sound casual. The sibling duo never had such serious conversations. But today, he felt the need for this discussion.

Shivangi continued, surprised and happy with her brother's participation in a discussion like this. "I realise how easy it would be to acknowledge this so-called privilege. We can form an opinion, we can make better choices, we can speak up for others, and we definitely can enjoy the lockdown at home without complaining."

"*Di*, you are right. Many of us have realised the value of this privilege. Still, human needs are never going to end. We are greedy for more. It is said, never should humans be satisfied with what they have, otherwise, how will they grow?" he replied with a little more enthusiasm, only to go back to staring at his mobile screen.

"Don't you think 'Satisfaction' is an underrated word? The more we dive deep into this word, the more we are enlightened. We can't compare if someone is more privileged, and the other is not. Being thankful towards life is the first step," Shivangi said.

"The society is unequal in every aspect. Looking at a poor kid craving food may bring tears to our eyes, but are we willing to come out of our comfort zones to help them?" Ayaansh asked.

She couldn't answer this question. They both stared at each other and went back to using their phones. Knowing that they were happy to talk about it but felt helpless when it came to practicality.

The next day Shivangi came across an article and couldn't stop herself from sharing her thoughts with her father.

Sanjay was sitting on the sofa in their living room, and she joined him.

"Papa, you know with privilege comes a lot of advantages. In March, Tom Hanks contracted coronavirus, and his privilege allowed for quick diagnosis and care. Meanwhile, so many others couldn't even get Covid-19 testing done. And I somehow feel grateful for the privilege we have. It is a blessing that we are safe at home."

"You have grown a lot, *beta*. It is indeed a blessing. But on the contrary, privilege can sometimes make you dull and dependent. Knowing we have someone to rely on makes us crave less, which can ultimately affect our growth as an individual. Sometimes, we become too egoistic to help anyone beneath us. That is scary for society. It might not be true for every individual, but it is for most people," he said as he took a sip of tea.

"The virus doesn't discriminate between anyone. Whether you are rich or poor," Shivangi said as she went back to her phone, looking for more articles. She found one that talked about a person faking to be an IAS officer to get the privileged treatment. She asked, shocked. "Papa, is it true that an IAS officer has extra privileges?"

"Yes, possibly, but why are you asking this?"

"I am reading this article. A man pretended to be an IAS officer to go on a drive. He had created a fake Id too," she spoke.

"I am not so surprised," Sanjay said, shaking his head in disapproval.

Shivangi continued, "Listen to this article, 'Police arrested a fake IAS during checking in Delhi's North-West District, who was on the road in his vehicle flouting the rules of the COVID-19 lockdown. According to the police, the Delhi Police logo was placed on the car of the accused when the vehicle was stopped at the barricade. The accused then got out of the car in anger and got entangled with the police. While flaunting, he described himself as Senior IAS in the

Ministry of Planets and said, 'how dare you check the car.' Government of India was also written on the back and front of the said car,'" she finished reading and looked at her father.

— (*Article Credits: DNA*-Daily News and Analysis)

"Can you believe it, Papa? Some people are taking these steps to roam around."

"I have to say, *beta*, these incidences clearly describe the need of a normal person to become 'someone' to enjoy specific rights. During the lockdown, someone like an IAS officer would only step out when it's necessary. They have a responsibility, yet we can't say if an individual would exploit their power," he said.

"Papa, but reaching such a higher post isn't easy," said Shivangi, surprised by her dad's explanation.

"Of course, becoming an IAS officer is a hard boat to row. It never comes easy. But after achieving that, no one would let go of something so precious earned by persistent hard work. The game of power, privilege, authority, and money has been played for years. It is not a new thing for us. But we never thought we'll have to experience all these in a pandemic," said her father with a smile on his face.

"But why do some people have to suffer more than the others?" Shivangi asked, expecting a different answer from him. Sanjay stayed silent for a while as if collecting his thoughts.

"It is because they are born there, and we are born here. Either we have worked hard to achieve this, or our parents did it for us. Our privilege is quite like chocolates and candies, not necessary, but keeps our life sweet."

COVID-19
VACCINE

2

FROM WHITE TO GREEN

It was a Sunday morning. Shivangi sat with her dad, having a cup of tea. The father-daughter duo loved spending the morning talking about anything and everything.

"Papa, for the people who have lost their loved ones, it is a pandemic. People who recovered from this virus consider it a disease. And for some who have only heard the news, it's just news and stats," Shivangi said in all seriousness.

"It's strange that the anchor of the news said the same thing yesterday. Did you write it after listening to him?" Sanjay asked in amusement. "I know from where you got these thoughts. Yesterday we were watching the news channel, and the anchor was saying the same thing. So, are you trying to fool me by saying it's your thought?"

"Fine!" she mumbled in defeat. "I heard it yesterday on the news. I liked the thought, so I wrote it down in my diary. And it's true."

"I agree. It is true."

"This pandemic hit us like the waves of the ocean. The strongest waves came together and took millions of lives. It may haunt us for years," she exclaimed.

"Yes, it might haunt us for a long time. The coming years won't be easy. Those who departed us were the clear victims of this monster. And the sufferings of the warriors fighting this will be unforgettable for their lifetime."

"The medical staff, the doctors, policemen, volunteers, and a lot of others who put their lives on the line to ensure that we, as a nation, are protected are the real heroes. Right, Papa?"

"Yes, of course, they are."

"But how are they so selfless about these things?"

"Because they chose to be. If you see from one perspective, it's the beauty in their heart. But from the other point of view, they are doing it for their livelihood."

"Isn't that unfair, Papa? I am sitting at home, and they are working, daily out there?" Shivangi asked.

"Nothing is fair, *beta*. Look at me now. If I have any work at the Airport, I will have to rush. I cannot escape my duties. The same thing implements to them as well," said Sanjay.

"So, duties are the priority in life doesn't matter who we are."

"Yes, *beta*, duty comes first."

Shivangi nodded. Talking to her father about this reminded her of Samaira and Swastik.

***

March 2020

The day after the nationwide lockdown was announced, Shivangi video called Samaira. They couldn't visit each other even after being neighbours.

"Hey, Shivangi," Samaira said. She had a pen in her hands, and her books were scattered on the floor.

"Oh, sorry, were you studying? Should I call later?" Shivangi asked. She knew medical studies were very tough. Both Diuja and Shivangi never disturbed Samaira during her study time.

"No, no. I was just taking a break," Samaira said as she closed her books and kept them aside.

"I can't believe what is happening!"

"Yes, me too. Everything in the country is closed," Samaira sighed.

"Even my college and tennis sessions are closed. Everything has restrictions now. And the scariest part is that so many people are dying," Shivangi said, panicked.

"Don't worry, bro. If people are dying, at least the population will decrease," Samaira said humorously.

"Bro, it is not funny. I mean it. I am scared."

"Don't get offended. You know I didn't mean it."

"I know, but still. Things are turning ugly. Anyhow, tell me, how was everything there?"

"It was pretty good, but you know, all of a sudden, we had to book tickets and rush home because of this outbreak. I am worried about my friends."

"Why are you worried about them?"

"They are working. The final year students and the interns have to work in the Covid wards in our college hospital."

"What? Are you serious? I mean, how will they work? They are not even skilled to that level," Shivangi almost shouted.

"Calm down, Shivangi. They are trained before they get to work in the hospital. Also, you only need to have basic knowledge about how to treat people with high fever and keep a check on the body temperature. Senior doctors are supervising them."

"So, they need to have the basic knowledge, and they can treat patients?"

"Yes, they are looking after them. Some of the interns had to go to different cities for the internship. Like my senior, Dr Swastik Ghare had an option between Pune and Aurangabad, so he chose Pune."

"Oh, but what is the need of the junior doctors like him to work for the Covid patients?"

"Because there is a shortage of doctors, the number of patients is increasing day by day, and the senior doctors aren't available everywhere. So, the medical teams are calling junior doctors, interns, and last year's students to treat the infected patients."

"So, only the last year's students, right? Like you are in the first year only. You obviously cannot work."

"Yes, only the last year ones. As I am in the first year only, I had to come home," she sadly added. "I wish I could switch places with Dr Swastik."

"What do you mean?"

"He is a senior of mine. He always helps me in every situation. In three months, we got close. He usually doesn't have much time, but he takes it for me. We text or talk on calls, especially when he is too stressed, he talks to me."

"You mean he is someone special?"

Samaira blushed, "No, it's nothing like that. We are only talking and have grown close. Everyone respects him in the college as he has been the General Secretary a lot of times. I am glad he talks to me about his life."

"Oh, I see what's going on. Are you guys dating?" Shivangi asked, and Samaira blushed again.

"No, we are not. We are close friends. Don't assume," Samaira swiftly waved her hand in denial.

"I can see you blushing, Samaira. Now come on, open up."

"Okay, fine. Honestly, nothing is going between us, but I do like him. Though, I don't know about him. I haven't confessed yet."

"Oh my god! That is such a huge thing, and you are telling me now."

"Well, nothing happened between us. I thought it was just a crush."

"Now I know why you are so concerned about him. You repeated his name quite a few times. So, does anyone else know?"

"Only my roommate Nandini, and you are the second person."

"You told her before me?" Shivangi exclaimed.

"Yes, because she was closer, and I didn't feel like sharing on the phone. Also, we are not even together or something. We are only talking, so how am I supposed to create a buzz about it."

"But still, it was important to share."

"Well, anyway, he is an ophthalmologist. I met him in the ophthalmology department. I had gone for my eye treatment, and he was the one checking the patients. He suggested that I should have eye surgery. I was not surprised, as you know, since a young age I have had an eye issue. He gave me his number and told me to contact him if I have further problems. I have known him for three months, but we got closer in the last month. We talked a lot, and now that this pandemic has hit us, things look different."

"How different? Tell me more about him. It kind of sounds like a fairy tale!" Shivangi said excitedly.

"It's nothing like that, bro. Also, it is different because now we are far away, and I miss him, even though I know we are not committed yet," Samaira sighed. "I should confess my feelings, but not now. I will let it happen naturally with the flow. And I hope it to be mutual."

"It is. Otherwise, why will he invest so much time in you?"

"You can say that." Samaira smiled as her face brightened up.

"Okay, so now tell me everything like where is he now?" Shivangi asked in excitement.

"Well, the situation is not good right now. That is why I am so worried. He lives in a flat in Aurangabad. Then a few days ago, before the pandemic started, he went to a hospital in Hyderabad for his training in ophthalmic surgery and his externship. When he reached there, the lockdown was executed all over the country."

"So, he had gone for an externship?"

"Yes, and now he is stuck there. As the people there speak Telugu and he comes from a Marathi background, it is tough for him to communicate with the patients. Moreover, most people there don't even speak English. To communicate, he spoke English to who understood it, and for the rest, he had to use sign language, which was quite a task."

"Oh, it seems like a lot of struggle."

"He is adapting now. He is smart enough. He has been there for a month now. Also, he is working there during the pandemic as he was called upon by the hospital authorities to treat the Coronavirus patients."

"Hats off to him and the other doctors like him. I wish he gets the strength to deal with all these."

"He will, but I still worry for him every day. Wearing a Personal protective equipment (PPE) kit every day. In twenty days, he had to prepare himself for the treatment of the Coronavirus infected patients."

"In twenty days?" Shivangi was surprised.

"Not only him, but other junior doctors who are not in the respiratory field had to treat the patients during this time of emergency. He is a junior doctor, 25 years of age, and is facing this pandemic for the very first time like us. Well, it's obvious for all the doctors facing this widespread pandemic."

"That's true. They are true heroes. So, what is his schedule?" Shivangi continued to ask, knowing her friend's probable date is a hardworking doctor.

"Initially, he had to work from seven to ten which is fifteen hours. It is unimaginable for a lot of us. But now it's ten in the morning to ten at night, which is twelve hours of work with forty minutes of lunch break in between."

"Samaira, fifteen hours while wearing the PPE kit? I definitely cannot imagine myself like that. The medical field is one of the toughest fields."

"I was shocked too when I came to know about his working hours, but I know how messy it can get. In the future, I may have to work such long hours too. I can relate to how mentally exhausting it can be. Not only him but many other junior doctors from different fields like researchers, orthopaedists, etc., are taking care of the Corona patients," Samaira said seriously.

Shivangi hummed in agreement as she grasped the level of dedication of the doctors.

"On the other hand, if we talk about the PPE kits, we have no idea how tough it is to handle. Even the quality sometimes of these kits is not well enough. The personal protective equipment kits include several items: a bodysuit, a pair of shoe cover, disposable goggles, gloves, disposable face mask, a collection in which they are meant to be discarded, and also a hand towel."

"I see. That could be suffocating."

"At first, he felt suffocated, but now he is habitual. You know, several of these items are often missing from the kits or are damaged, needing them to use crude, quick-fix solutions like adhesives. Wearing a PPE kit for around fifteen hours in a hospital for an entire day with fewer breaks and attending the Covid 19 patients is a tough row to hoe."

Samaira shook her head and shrugged as she continued, "Well, that was the time when he was in Hyderabad. He came back to Maharashtra a few days ago."

"And when were you planning to tell me?" Shivangi asked annoyingly.

"You said you wanted to know everything, so I am explaining you from the very start."

"Oh, like a story, or should I say a love story?" Shivangi teased Samaira.

"Shut up, Shivangi," Samaira said as she blushed.

"I can see you are blushing," she teased again.

"Do you want to hear about him or not?"

"Yes. Yes. Please continue."

"So, as he shifted back to Maharashtra. He went to Pune, where his family resides, and during this time, he was concerned about his dad as he has high blood pressure (hypertension) and he needed to take care of him."

"I see."

"He stays away from his family when he goes to the hospital. All the working doctors and nurses are most concerned about their families. They prefer to stay isolated during these kinds of situations."

"So, where is he staying?" Shivangi asked.

"He had a flat rented there when he was doing his internship. His friends who stay with him have gone to stay with their respective families. He lives all alone, as he chooses to stay isolated and away from his family. Furthermore, every day

around 150 patients turn up to the hospital for their treatment."

"Wow, he has to work a lot. So, when does he get time to talk to you?" Shivangi asked in a rush. She was very excited to know how Swastik got time from his busy schedule to talk to Samaira.

"Only at night. When he comes back home all exhausted. He still gives me around one hour from eleven to twelve. He talks to me and takes everything out. He says he loves talking to me, he feels much better, and I am more than happy to talk to him. Every night I wait for his texts. It is like exclusively our time. Also, sometimes he does text me between his shifts during his breaks or something, but not for long."

"Oh, this thing has gone too far. You guys are behaving like a committed couple."

"No, we are not."

"I can see it; you both are into each other."

"Maybe, but for now, I am more worried for his mental health."

"Oh yes. It may have led to a drastic change in his mental health. From a junior ophthalmologist to a doctor treating the Covid-19 patients, it's not a piece of cake," Shivangi exclaimed.

"There are many like him, whether it's a senior or a junior doctor. They are always working. There's no lockdown for them or even a holiday, especially during this time of emergency. It is the toughest and most demanding time for medical professionals around the world. Even after so much mental stress and physical changes, he said that he loves his profession," Samaira smiled and continued. "I remember his text messages where he said, 'I love working no matter what it is, how stressful or risky. I got a first-hand experience, and that's something I will cherish. From the professional front, it will help me in the future,'" she said proudly.

Samaira couldn't stop gushing about Dr Swastik. She told Shivangi how he had once mentioned his mental state. He talked about how his lifestyle has been widely affected. He is not able to give time to his friends and family. One day, when his father went to buy the essentials. After coming home, he was continuously coughing and felt weak. That time Swastik felt so vulnerable and selfish that he wanted to leave his duties and go back to his family, but his mother took care of his dad. Luckily, it wasn't Covid.

"It was so tough for him to choose between his family and his duty, but as a doctor, you have to make tough decisions," Samaira said, almost on the verge of tears.

"Well, I can see how these doctors progressed from being scared to being responsible for their duties. Their journey has not been easy. They all have won our hearts; they are determined to overcome this deadly virus with all their strengths as they are a true blessing to us. I am thankful for a doctor like Swastik, and I understand your worries about his health. After all, he is one of the most important people in your life, right?" Shivangi teased her again, trying to lighten her mood.

"Yes, he is," Samaira accepted gracefully and smiled back at her.

"Well, I remember one time when he treated a patient with all the symptoms of this virus. He didn't have the required protective gear. He was so scared about getting infected that he couldn't sleep at night," she added.

"What had happened?"

"He had a mild fever when he woke up the next morning. He then had some medicines, took some rest, and isolated himself. Thankfully, he was all fine in the next two days and didn't have any symptoms, so there was no need for a test. I freaked out when he told me about this."

Shivangi could see the worry in her friend's eyes.

"I know it is his duty, but he is not taking care of his health. He eats less the whole day. His dinner is almost always bread or chips. He avoids grocery shopping as he gets too tired after the shifts and wants to get isolated and handle everything by himself. He reaches his flat at around eleven at night. He has no energy left to cook anything at that time."

"How does he only eat chips and bread?"

"He cooks his breakfast himself in the morning, which is mostly omelette bread, French toast, or fruits. For lunch, he takes the tiffin, which is very prominent in Maharashtra. Sometimes, he misses his lunch due to his duties."

"Seriously, bro, I am also concerned about him now. Tell him to take care of himself."

"I remind him every single day to take care of himself. His life had turned from white to green when he used to wear his white coat without much pressure to now stressing out every day, his life turned green," Samaira said and looked down. "He is sacrificing, compromising, learning, growing in every way, but most importantly, he is fighting. He went from his normal routine as an ophthalmologist to the fear of his family getting contaminated. He had a lot of changes cognitively."

"I want to know, if they choose this life, I mean to have such a hectic life, treating patients, prioritizing your duties. I mean, all this is not easy, right?" Shivangi asked, raising her eyebrows. After knowing how a doctor's life can take a turn, she was concerned for her to-be-doctor friend.

"Well, if you are asking me, then yes. I would love to save lives as I love challenges, and what's the meaning of life if it's not tough or challenging enough? I want to treat patients with utmost courage and patience in the future. I might get nervous,
but this is what I want from my life," Samaira said proudly.

"I am proud to hear that, bro. The truth is only a doctor is blessed with the magic to be there with us when we have lost all hopes. This world has become a better and healthier place to live in with doctors bringing joy and goodness to our lives," said Shivangi.

"Above all, the doctors are ready to face any tough challenge coming their way, and their lives are never easy. They do noble work and have loyalty towards their patients. It is a rare profession where 'trust' is the most important factor for the individuals associated with this field. Saving the lives of fellow citizens is their mere duty. That is the beauty of their life," Samaira replied.

They kept talking for a little more while when both were called for dinner by their families.

"Coming," they both shouted at the same time and laughed about it.

"Now, I will have to go. It's already late, but I know you are excited for tonight."

"Okay, stop it. Now go," Samaira couldn't resist but blushed again.

Shivangi cut the call and fell back to her bed. She was overwhelmed when she realised how these doctors- young ones and seniors, nurses, even the last year students, everyone in the medical field were working hard to curb this virus.

***

Present

After that conversation, both Samaira and Shivangi haven't talked for a while. Shivangi thought of checking up on Swastik, so she called Samaira, who picked in a second. She was playing with Pulu. She signalled Shivangi to wait for a second as she held up her index finger and put the phone in a stable platform. She picked up Pulu and went outside the room. After a while, she came back. They both sat down to chat. Shivangi asked her about Dr Swastik, and she told her about him.

"You know, Swastik and I were talking on the call yesterday. He got to know about a three-year-old little girl from his colleagues during his break."

"What happened?" Shivangi sounded tense.

"There is a small girl in Karnataka. Both her parents died due to Covid a few days ago. They were hospitalised, so they left the child with their neighbours. None of their family members lived in the same city. All the other relatives are in Delhi. The Father died after fourteen days of hospitalization, and then the mother died too. They both got beds in the hospital, but they could not survive. The most heart-breaking part is that the neighbours tried to hide that fact from the little girl. But after a few days, she understood, and now she's in shock. Can you believe a three-year-old kid is going through this?"

"Oh my God! That is so bad. I feel so sorry for the girl."

"This is the saddest news I heard, and he has to hear these stories almost every day. He cannot sleep at night sometimes, especially when he comes to know that one of his patients had died, he starts blaming himself."

"This must be so hard for him," Shivangi said sadly.

"It turns into a nightmare for him," Samaira said and continued.

"The irony is, no matter how hard doctors work, people still blame them. They don't understand that the doctors are already in so much pain. I know hospital bills can get expensive, but that doesn't mean doctors are at fault. A Doctor's job is to treat the patients, for God's sake!" Samaira exclaimed in anger.

"This is so disturbing. I see in the media the problems doctors are facing. People are getting violent. I saw the news last month about how people were throwing stones at doctors. They even spat on them."

"Exactly. Why don't people understand that doctors are risking their own lives to save them? Yet they are the ones badly treated."

"I know. I hope people understand this and let the doctors do their duties."

"You know the thing is, everyone should have the basic knowledge of medical examination. For example, how to check the pulse rate. People don't have much idea about these things, which is why there are a lot of deaths. The lack of awareness is the issue," Samaira ranted. "Anyhow, I am glad nothing of this sort has happened to Swastik. But still, he is working with his life on risk."

"I want to talk to him once and pay respect to him for working endlessly for us," Shivangi said in admiration.

3

IMMUNITY

While she was still on call, Shivangi got a text from Diuja. She remembered that Diuja's younger sister was not well. She couldn't resist sharing this with Samaira.

"You know, Diuja's cousin sister is in the hospital right now. She is around eight years old. She had Covid a few days ago and had already recovered. One day she couldn't stop coughing, had a slight fever, and had a breathing problem. Then they understood the issue.

"Her parents took her to the hospital. The doctors prescribed some medicines and assured her that she would be fine. They came back home in the evening. But at night, she had a breathing problem again, so she was admitted. They kept her in observation for three to four days. She was kept on glucose with so much intensive care as if she was in the ICU. Diuja said it happened because she had a lot of antibodies in her body as this is what the doctor said," Shivangi said.

"I see. Children's immune systems are much stronger than ours. They develop antibodies much better than us. It is due to cytokines produced by several immune cells. It can happen to anyone, not only kids. The enzymes in our body fight the virus, and due to excess white blood cells, it's like a war between the virus and the immune system, and the body cannot take it. Too much virus interaction will start affecting the oxygen in the body, which may lead to death. You know, sixty percent of people suffering from Covid are dying due to cytokines in their bodies."

"Oh, now I got it, doctor. A lot of antibodies can harm you too. It is equal to a virus. Coming to immunity, I know you don't exercise, then how do you maintain your immunity?" Shivangi asked.

Shivangi knew Samaira would never even think of exercising. She studies for hours and has never been so fond of fitness. For her, eating is more important than moving her body.

"Yes, and please, don't call me a doctor. I am still a student. Exercise is not the only way to keep your immunity strong. I eat good and healthy food for my immunity. I take Vitamin C and zinc tablets as well."

"I know you are still a student, but for me, you are my personal junior doctor. And even I take Vitamin C & zinc tablets nowadays, but for me exercising is more important," she sighed.

Remembering the time when she used to step out to work out at the gym and play tennis tournaments around the country, Shivangi felt a bit upset. Now she had to work out at her home, without much assistance. She was preparing for her examinations when the lockdown was announced, and her exams were cancelled. She had come after winning a tournament. Soon she got to know there wouldn't be any more tennis tournaments for now. All the sports academies were closed due to the pandemic. No one was allowed to even step out of their houses. Being a fitness enthusiast, she exercised daily.

"During this pandemic, we need to take care of our immunities. Why don't you start to work out? I will instruct you. We can do it together. What say?" Shivangi asked enthusiastically, though she already knew what the answer would be.

"You know me. I won't. I am anyways too lazy for all these physical activities. Besides, I have a lot of other things to do rather than working out. You should go and exercise, but I have to study," Samaira said to which Shivangi nodded and cut the call.

Looking at her confidence, Shivangi couldn't utter a single word.

"I don't understand why people do not care about their health," she loudly exclaimed as she walked out of her room. Her father, who was still sitting on the sofa, heard her.

"Why waste your energy when you know you can't change them. It's better to relax and focus on your life. People will have to suffer for their deeds one day," he explained calmly.

The father-daughter duo exercised in the evening. Amita worked out in the morning, and Ayaansh was the only one not doing any physical exercise. He would spend the whole day playing games on his computer.

"Yes, you are right, Papa. I shouldn't waste my energy on people, stubborn enough to stick to their old lifestyles. I mean, look at our own house. Ayaansh never exercises either."

Listening to this, Ayaansh came out of his room, and both brother and sister started arguing. Ayaansh stated how he was already fit, and Shivangi dismissed it as a lame excuse. That went on until their mother served their favourite food on the table. And said with finality in her tone, "You guys will only get to eat this paneer chilli if you stop arguing."

They both looked at the dish, stared at each other, and rushed towards it to have the first bite.

"We can have these homemade dishes, but not every day. It is for our weekend cravings. During this time, we'll have to drink fresh *Giloy* juice with hot water every day in the morning to boost our immunities. We will have more fruits and vegetables in our diet consisting of more nutrients. We will have multivitamin tablets too. All of us will have to follow these strictly," said her mother in a dominating tone while they enjoyed the yummy dish.

After enjoying the delicious food, Shivangi spent the day writing, reading, and helping her mom. In the evening, she had a great workout session with her dad. When Shivangi was going to sleep, she remembered that Diuja had messaged her earlier. She went back to her room and found her phone on the bed. She immediately video called Diuja. It took her a while to pick up. As soon as she picked up, Shivangi could hear Diuja's younger siblings shouting, and she was trying her best to shush them. Shivangi laughed at her misery but immediately shut up when she glared at her. Diuja then asked her siblings to leave the room, which of course, they ignored until she threatened to eat all their chocolates. Once her siblings left the room, she shut the door, sat on the bed, and relaxed. She was so tired and was about to fall asleep when she heard Shivangi.

"Hello. Bro, where are you?"

"Oh, sorry, I forgot. I am so tired. These little monsters have tortured me the whole day."

"It's ok," Shivangi laughed, and Diuja smiled too.

"Anyways, you say, what's going on?"

"Nothing. How are you? And your cousin sister?"

"She is better now. She got home now. And I am so happy to be back on the bed," Diuja said as she yawned and stretched a little.

"Yes. The cases are increasing. We are lucky enough to stay at our homes safely," said Shivangi.

Diuja knew from Shivangi's face that something was bothering her. When Diuja asked, she told all about Samaira and Ayaansh not exercising. Diuja laughed about it for a minute, and it was Shivangi's turn to glare. Diuja then seriously said,

"There are various ways to stay healthy at home. Studies show having enough sleep is one of them. Meditating is an obvious way to stay calm. Avoiding caffeine and your diet matters too."

Shivangi understood her perspective.

"And sleeping is love! Also, I know how diet-conscious you are. The lockdown has allowed us to stay at our homes and spend time with our families. To enjoy and relax for a bit," Diuja said and rested her head on the bed.

"But some of them have become lazier. Their whole routine is changed. Some are enjoying this time without any stress. That's a good thing indeed, but not taking care of our health and endlessly eating is not a good habit," Shivangi said as she relaxed too.

"Eating homemade food is good, but if we don't move our body, it will tend to become heavier, which in the long term affects our health."

"I agree. I heard about an obese man who died due to Covid-19 in my aunt's building. He never cared to exercise or follow a proper diet. He already had diabetes, and his immunity wasn't strong enough," Shivangi said as she got a little upset.

"That is so sad but true. There are a lot of cases like this. On the contrary, I have seen sportspersons, healthy and fit, fighting this virus in a better way."

"Yes, a lot of my friends have recovered in a few days because they all are fit. Being in sports helped them in dealing with this. I miss playing tennis, going to the tournaments, working out on the ground. Although, I am now habitual to doing yoga and meditation at home. Some days, I skip meditation but have never skipped my workout routine. After all, it is what keeps me active," Shivangi said in enthusiasm.

"Your routine is great. Keep it up. I, however, have become lazy as I don't have any schedule, nor do I exercise. I remember when I used to play tennis, I was much fitter and now look at me with all such fat. I have seen so many fitter bodies on social media, it motivates me, but at the same time, I feel low when I compare myself to them," Diuja said, sounding a bit low.

Shivangi replied immediately, "Never compare yourself with anyone. It will kill your happiness. You can start any day. In fact, I can help you to make sure you come to a good shape and eat the proper diet."

As usual, Shivangi volunteered to help someone she cared about.

Diuja nodded as Shivangi continued, "Our mental health is important for now. My mother keeps scolding me for stressing about my academics during this time. She says the competition is not about who works the hardest and wins. It is about who can survive by taking the needed precautions and staying healthy."

"You are right. Being mentally healthy is the priority. Okay, I won't stress and will focus on the positive side. I will focus on health and won't chase body standards. Thank you for always motivating me," Diuja gave a grateful smile. Shivangi dismissed her thank you with a wave of her hand.

Thank you and sorry were the rare words seldom used between these best friends, but the pandemic had taught them to be grateful for every person and thing.

They both continued to talk for a while until more yawns were shared than words, and they decided to go and sleep.

The next morning, Shivangi had just finished her breakfast when her dietician Dr Heenal, texted to check on her. Before the pandemic started, Shivangi had gone for a diet regime with her for three months. She decided to call her, as she wanted her suggestions during these times. Being an extrovert somehow helped her in communicating with others. She had a friendly relationship with Dr Heenal. Shivangi never felt awkward with her.

"Hello, Ma'am. Good morning, how are you doing? I hope you are not busy; I don't want to disturb you."

"Hello *beta*, I am doing well. How are you? How's everything at home? I hope you all are safe. No, I am not busy as I am working from home, as you may know," she laughed.

"I am good; we all are safe. Yes, we are also not stepping out of our houses. Work from home is the new lifestyle, I guess," Shivangi laughed too.

"Yes, it is. I am helping my clients through video calls. I am telling you. It was tough for me initially to guide them on the screen, but I have adapted it finally. Anyways, how's your diet going? Are you eating healthy?"

"I have food made at home though I am not monitoring much. I am not restricting myself from eating a particular food. As mom has told us to eat whatever is available during these times. I am shedding the extra calories through workouts, and I have enough protein in my diet."

"It's good to know, *beta*; keep it up. Stay active and keep having a healthy diet. Eating the right food is very important. All the medical and Ayurveda experts suggest exercising regularly, sleeping enough, and having a healthy diet, especially during this time. The question is, what percentage of people follow this? There is still a stubborn population who doesn't care to follow," she said a few things that Shivangi already knew.

"You have patients who are healthier now, right?"

"Yes, but not all of them follow the diet plan given to them. They all have more cheat days than workouts. In our country, the percentage of people like this is too high, which is the cause of chronic diseases. It's high time, especially during this pandemic, to make a change in our lifestyle," said Dr Heenal in a very calm voice.

"Yes. That's true, ma'am. Until everyone is not immune against this virus, how will this pandemic come to an end?" Shivangi said,

"There are studies which show that we must start planning for a permanent solution. Going back wouldn't be an option; the only way is forward. But to what exactly? We don't know yet," Dr Heenal added in a bit more serious tone.

"If the pandemic remains here for a long time, it will get tougher for us to get back a normal life. In our twenties, we are sitting at our homes. Colleges are nowhere close to reopening. People are dying in high numbers. Isn't there any solution for this pandemic?" asked Shivangi curiously.

"Well, they are saying most epidemics disappear once populations achieve herd immunity. And for that, all the people in the community should have strong immunity to fight this virus. We shouldn't only depend on the vaccines. We need to spread awareness about good nutrition and active lifestyle."

"But not everyone gets that exposure in our country like the poor. Although I have seen a lot of people moulding themselves into healthy and good habits due to the fear of these circumstances."

"Yes, right. Fear drives people to stay active and change their eating habits. Though, people give good excuses for not following an exercise routine. Regular exercise is essential under normal circumstances and especially crucial during the pandemic," Dr Heenal explained with her whole heart.

"Yes, it's true. Our habits mould our lifestyle and the future. I had heard about Indians having a good immunity compared to the other countries. What do you think?" Shivangi continued asking questions.

"Several cases are coming up, and looking at the population of India, it is tough to control the spread of the virus. It is possible theoretically as we Indians are exposed to microbes that keep our immune system primed and destroy pathogens. That's why children in a clean environment fall sick at the slightest exposure to a pathogen—a concept known as the hygiene hypothesis. We Indians have some advantages, but after all, it's a pandemic, and to survive, we need to follow the given guidelines and take care of our health," she sighed.

"Yes, ma'am, you are right. The statistic of our country is poor if we look at the number of people who exercise, compared to other countries like Japan, Canada, and Switzerland," said Shivangi with utmost confidence. She felt good knowing a little stat about the country.

"Yes, you are right, *beta*. Various studies and reports show that many patients who recovered from the coronavirus and tested negative later tested positive again. Many patients that recovered from the virus suffer post-Covid complications. It becomes difficult for them to live the same old life," said Dr Heenal with a pause.

Shivangi took in everything that Dr Heenal said.

"We all should learn from the countries like Japan. They follow a cluster-based approach. The 'Japan Model' of combating Covid 19 has been successful, at least to this point. I liked the country's approach to the pandemic. Any physical contact like shaking hands, hugging, and kissing is not part of the traditional Japanese greetings. Other factors also include the healthy and less eating habits of Japanese. They always eat boiled food and have green tea. They try to avoid fast food as much as possible, and they prefer to walk rather than use a vehicle. I like that country's routine." Dr Heenal paused for breath. "These are the reasons why Japan has handled the pandemic well compared to the other countries despite having a high population of senior citizens. They have faced pandemics earlier too, so they are always ready."

"I agree with that. Also, in India, people living in slums are already exposed to an unhealthy environment. Hence the immune system gets strong. Yet, somewhere, we all have fallen psychologically," Shivangi said.

"Being mentally strong is the most important thing. It is indeed true. A lot of people are getting anxious and panicking, which is obvious. People are losing their livelihood. How will they even get the hope to live? That is the major reason why people are giving up."

"Let's pray for the best, ma'am. Thank you so much for your insights. I learned a lot of things from you today. Please stay safe and take care of yourself and your family. Have a nice day, ma'am," Shivangi said in a hurry as she knew she had taken a lot of time from Dr Heenal's busy schedule.

"Yes, I will. You, too, take care of yourself and your loved ones. Remember to always keep your morale high, *beta*. Have a nice day, stay strong and safe," Dr Heenal said as she hung up.

Shivangi was awestruck by the wonderful conversation. She had learned so much and wanted to share with her family and friends, but for now, she chose to write everything in her book. She started on a new page with the title 'immunity' and then noted her thoughts.

"This pandemic has taught the whole world the importance of health more than wealth. The theory of health and wealth is proven right. It is the primary need to survive in this world. Globally powerful and economically strong countries couldn't handle the pandemic well enough compared to smaller countries. It is a lesson to the whole world that only power, authority, and money are not important to survive a pandemic like this. The main key is effective leadership, which shows that unity is the key."

4

SOCIAL MEDIA CIRCUS

Shivangi spent most of her days writing, talking to her friends, or scrolling Instagram. The thing she liked the most was connecting with friends she hadn't talked to for years. Everyone had enough time in the lockdown to get in touch with their long-lost friends. Shivangi connected with a lot of her friends and got closer to a few. But today, Ricky's message made her lose her calm. Ricky and Shivangi met during a tennis tournament and instantly hit it off. Ricky was a tennis player, but as lockdown started, she couldn't continue her tennis practice. So, she leaned towards one thing a lot of people were leaning on- Instagram. She wanted to be an influencer, the fashion queen. She spent most of her time making reels hoping to get thousands of views. She started comparing herself with other girls, who shared their most "perfect" pictures.

"Why does this happen to me, Shivangi?" asked Ricky trying not to sound anxious.

"You shouldn't overthink, Ricky. It is only a platform to share a part of your life. You don't have to compare yourself with others."

Shivangi somewhere knew this would happen. She was aware of Ricky's growing addiction to social media.

"Yes, I know, but I don't feel good if I don't post anything."

This behaviour of Ricky always annoyed her, but she tried to be calm.

"You shouldn't think about what others think about you," she tried not to sound blunt.

"You are right. I shouldn't worry, but don't you think I can do better when it comes to content?"

Ricky constantly sought validation from her friends. The continuous efforts of becoming a social media influencer took a toll on her mental health. Her happiness depended on her Instagram posts, and all the hurt came from there, too. Shivangi had realised this, as she thought, *why do you need to show everything to people out there? Privacy is a privilege nowadays.* However, she couldn't say these things to Ricky as she knew it would hurt her.

"You cannot always be the best. Just focus on your uniqueness," Shivangi typed.

"I don't think I am good enough," read the reply.

Shivangi kept her phone away, got up, and went to Ayaansh. She knew she could share this stuff with him.

"Ricky is too influenced by the social media world. How am I supposed to help her? She is drowning in it!" She exclaimed.

"Calm down, *Di*. What happened?" He asked, startled.

"She constantly asks me if she looks perfect in her posts."

"And what's wrong with that?"

"She asks a lot. I get irritated. I am tired of explaining that it doesn't matter in the real world. She is addicted to it. I don't even want to reply to her texts anymore," Shivangi ranted.

"It's okay, *Di*. You need to understand her point of view too."

"What point of view?" she raised her eyebrows.

"Like if she is happy in that thing, let her be."

"Being happy is different, and obsessing over it is different, Ayaansh. It is affecting her mental health negatively, and it is disturbing me, too."

"Then maintain a distance. You cannot do anything, *Di*."

"Don't you think, Ayaansh, we have reached a point where everything revolves around social media? Jokes, memes, trending music, and even news."

"Obviously. For instance, check my meme page. Everything has changed," Ayaansh said calmly, his eyes on the computer. He was completing his HTML project. His exam dates kept postponing, and he didn't want to waste time at home. So, Ayaansh and his best friend Veer joined some online classes.

"Are you even listening?"

"I am. Keep talking."

"The time has changed so much. Everything is connected through technology, whether it's a good match on dating apps or finding jobs on LinkedIn."

"Dating app, huh?" he teased her.

"Stop it, Ayaansh. I am only giving an example," she said while Ayaansh smirked at her.

"Don't smile like that," Shivangi warned.

"See, *Di*, we all know, social media has both pros and cons. So, look at the bright side too. During this pandemic, we can easily get all the updates on social media. It is playing an important role for us. I was talking to Veer, and I remembered all our fun together. We all are feeling isolated. I know we all will meet again, but we don't know when. So, for now, the most fun thing is creating memes together for our page," he defended.

"I understand, Ayaansh. We all want that. Even I want to meet Diuja. But we are adapting to this environment. Life in lockdown is not that tough as we imagined it to be."

Ayaansh looked at her and smiled, "I know. And it's because we have smartphones with us. We are scrolling Instagram every day. You keep checking your Facebook too."

"I don't use Facebook," she said, irritated.

"You use it."

"No, I use Instagram more. I don't use Facebook a lot," she defended again.

"But at least you use it. I don't even have an account on it."

"So, what's the big deal? We can't forget Netflix and other OTT platforms. You are the one spending all your time on those."

"So, I don't spend all my time gossiping and stalking people on Instagram. I watch educational movies and gain knowledge. It's not called wasting time," he said in his defence.

"Oh, really, name a few educational movies then. All you watch is action. And keep playing or video games or making not at all funny memes."

"Oh, please, you know nothing about memes," Ayaansh told her off.

"See, just like Ricky, any person scrolling through these apps and looking at others doing different stuffs has all led to a competition among netizens which can be unhealthy and toxic. I feel like the joy of doing stuff you never tried and sharing it on social media is not wrong. But people are greedier for likes rather than enjoying the process," Shivangi said in all seriousness.

"You are right, *Di*. I think it is the craving for attention. However, people do it for their happiness too."

"Okay, I agree. If we see pictures of fitness, baking, or any other activity, it may motivate us to do the same. But at the same time, for some people, when the result is not what they want, it leads to mental stress," she paused. She was standing beside Ayaansh; she walked to the bed, sat down, and continued. "The question is, where have we reached? People invest their energy into content according to the trend and not what they enjoy. And I don't at all understand this social media circus."

Before Ayaansh could speak, she interrupted again, "See, this is the truth."

Ayaansh shook his head in displeasure and continued to work on his computer. Shivangi knew that she was being adamant, but still, she continued, "The point is, today, even a kid studying in school knows the latest trends. Anyone can get attention and fame through these platforms. The talented ones can get viral and appreciated, while others could do something different to get noticed by the netizens. Isn't it too easy nowadays?" she questioned.

"But it is not this generation's fault. The facilities we are enjoying are all due to the change in this world. Each layer of change peels off the old living style and reveals a whole new world to us."

Even though Shivangi understood his point, she still thought of how negative these platforms' impact can be. Though everyone shares their life experiences, they never show their true selves on these platforms. *In today's world, how tough is it to be a vulnerable person? The fear of being laughed at has created a fake world on these platforms. No one shares their failures on the social media platforms,* she thought.

"*Di*, everything is available under your nose when it comes to technology," Ayaansh spoke and brought Shivangi out of her thoughts.

"The obvious thing is that we can't underestimate social media. Though again, everything has its cons, right? The major impact which can happen during a pandemic is the misinformation."

He smiled and shook his head again, clearly disagreeing with her. Ayaansh got up and went to the kitchen to fetch a glass of water, and Shivangi followed him.

"This debate has dried my throat. I need water," he filled a glass of water for himself and even offered her one, but she shook her head and continued speaking. "Coming to misinformation, the rumours spread through the digital platforms, like WhatsApp. Connectivity has surely impacted in a good and a huge way, but most problems happen due to miscommunication. Look at our family group, how our aunts and uncles keep sending irrelevant messages related to Covid."

"They have nothing better to do. That's why it is called the WhatsApp University. We have to ignore them and keep filtering," Ayaansh said. He finished his glass of water and went back to his room as she followed again.

"Yes, but did you see what aunt Ruby sent that day about these medicines by an unknown brand which will save you from coronavirus. Wasn't it funny?" Shivangi mocked her aunt.

"Of course, I saw, but we won't follow it. People keep sending me different solutions every day. Some are relevant, but not all of them. One of my friends sent me a mantra to read every day to stay away from the virus. Even though I believe in God, this is stupid."

"Believing in God and praying is a strong thing but chanting a particular mantra every day without taking any precautions is nothing but useless..." Shivangi said.

As she was still talking, Ayaansh abruptly sat down in a cross-legged pose and started chanting, "Go corona. Go corona. Go corona."

Shivangi was startled at first, but soon they both burst off laughing. After a while, they relaxed, and sat on the bed. The mood had lightened, but when Ayaansh saw Shivangi in deep thought again, he sighed.

"*Di*, these are a few things, but what about its usage? Some people found plasma donors through the internet. There are pages created to help find oxygen cylinders, donation groups, volunteers, and whatnot," Ayaansh said softly.

"I am not saying it is bad. But I am tired of some people bothering too much."

"Then you have to ignore them. It's the only solution. In today's world, medical health has advanced due to technology. What would have happened if the pandemic had occurred hundred years ago, like the Spanish flu? I saw a video about this. So many people died because there was no way to communicate with other countries, which created major chaos. So, we should be thankful for these advancements," he continued.

"I agree with you, but people who degrade themselves due to social media standards sometimes fall into depression, and in a few cases, it leads to suicide."

Ayaansh raised his eyebrows, and Shivangi countered confidently, "What? I have researched about it."

"Not all the things spread negativity. There is some positivity too. Look at the mass of people supporting each other. Medical staff spreading awareness through these platforms. These are some of the good things to look at, *Di*."

"Well, you are right," Shivangi went into a soft tone and changed her narrative. "The social media platforms are not all bad. It is true that in the most difficult times, it has helped us to reach others. The doctors got huge support during these hard times. People connected with others all around the globe and even sent their condolences and helped those in need. It is a big family of all the humans living in the world. We cannot even imagine our situation if there would not have been the internet, smartphones, and these social media apps. It has become a part of our lives. More than an addiction; it is the need."

"Exactly, the technology, *Di*. Finally, you understood what I was trying to say," Ayaansh said with excitement in his eyes.

"I already knew, but I was talking about its ill effects, and whether this is bad or good, only time will tell," Shivangi sniggered.

"Time keeps changing. Nowadays, we can check the number of cases with a click of our fingers. Various apps developed specifically to tackle this pandemic has helped too. We all are far away but still close to each other all due to the technology," said Ayaansh positively.

"Yes, the lack of awareness, knowledge, and preparation can put people and the health care at risk. And social media has helped change people's behaviour and promote the well-being of individual and public health. Also, I have seen so many videos of doctors and policemen on Instagram dancing and spreading awareness in such a fun way," she said. Ayaansh finally felt like her sister understood his point. He stood up and went back to his computer.

"Exactly. Look at the brighter side. Today, we sit in front of the screens, sipping coffee and watching all that is happening in the world. Even online classes and official meetings have turned into virtual video conferencing calls. All thanks to technology," he gushed.

"Yes, I know. And talking about virtual connectivity, do you even attend your classes?" Shivangi asked.

"Of course, I do!"

"Don't lie. I know you don't. You play games on the computer during your classes."

"Not every day. I just completed my project."

"Yes, because today was the deadline."

Ayaansh looked at his elder sister in annoyance.

"What? I am telling the truth," she defended.

"You are correct. So, can we pause your lecture now? And if your highness could please leave my room," he said sarcastically.

"Yes. Yes," Shivangi couldn't help but had to leave. She knew she had troubled him enough.

Shivangi was still a little irritated by Ricky's continuous whining about each and everything she posted. She realised the depth of social media obsession people could have. But she sat in her room and thought about her conversation with Ayaansh. She tried to understand Ricky's point of view too. In this time of crisis, when people are affected by loneliness, they turn to various sources to find happiness and validation. And even though Shivangi didn't like

Ricky's choice, she understood that she was just another person seeking help from her friends.

On the other hand, she understood how technology has evidently changed lives. Almost everything is digitalised, whether it is the E-boarding passes, E-tickets, E-education, or Cashless payments.

"The availability of everything on small screens has been a huge change in everyone's lives," Shivangi mumbled to herself.

OXYGEN

5

WHERE ARE WE HEADING?

It was mid-June; Shivangi kept her writing going. She worked out daily too. But the environment was getting tense. One night, Shivangi couldn't sleep. She couldn't stop but think about all those things happening around her. She watched the latest news on television, read the newspapers, scrolled through social media, and saw that almost everyone had a sad story to tell. She distracted herself by studying and preparing for the entrance exams, which may not happen anytime soon.

It is important to preserve your mental health. But can we run away from reality? We cannot escape the truth about what's happening around us, she thought. She kept thinking the whole night, and it was hard for her to wake up early the next morning.

Even as she got out of bed, her first thought was, *have people changed with time? Or were they the same before too? Everything isn't the same again; things have changed. We have become so selfish that we have left humanity behind.*

She was disturbed and wanted to distract herself. And as always, she chose to scroll through Instagram, where she got to know that one of her close friends, Riya, had recently come back from the US, where she was doing her bachelors. Shivangi messaged her, and Riya responded instantly. After texting for a while, they decided to switch to a phone call as they had not talked in a very long time and texting was too tedious.

"Hey. How are you?" Riya asked.

"I am fine, Riya, you say, long time no see."

"I came from the US a few days ago. Everything has been so hectic."

"Oh, what happened? You sound so exhausted."

"What do I say? My travelling experience was so bad. I feel like I had come back from hell."

"Oh!" Shivangi was stunned to hear her speak like that. Riya was a very patient person, and if something could disturb her to this extent, it had to be huge.

"So, as you know, I was having trouble getting any flight to come back. I was stuck there for the last three months, from March to May. I had a very pathetic experience. These times have been challenging for me," she sighed. "I got the news that a virus has arrived in the US, several people got affected in Texas, and some of them died within eight hours. We were all scared, and it shook me to the core. Within weeks, it started to spread, and in no time, it was all over the world. All international flights were cancelled in India."

"I know. It was the need of the hour."

"It was, but it resulted in a lot of trouble for me. When the virus was spreading initially, there were no masks, sanitisers, hand gloves, or anything required for precautions. The production was less, and the stock went directly to the hospitals, so people like us weren't getting these supplies. I was scared to even step out of the house. Even small sanitiser bottles and masks were expensive in the US. Most of the time, it wasn't even available in the pharmacy."

"You didn't ask the store owners about the supply of these products? For buying it later."

"I used to ask them, but they usually would say that they don't know when the stock will refill. It was too scary for me, Shivangi. I was planning to come since March, but they had already started online classes, and my semester ended in May."

"So, how did you come back?"

"I heard about the *Vande Bharat* Mission. I applied for it immediately, but you know how many people would have applied for it too. So, I didn't get the seat the first time. I reapplied and waited for a few more days when finally, my ticket was confirmed by the Air India airlines. Trust me; the experience was so bad. I cannot stop cursing them."

"Was it really that bad?" Shivangi asked. She thought Riya was over exaggerating. Even Shivangi's father worked at the airport, and she knew how hard the aviation industry works.

Riya chuckled, "This was the worst travelling experience of my life. First, they charged a hell lot of money. It was too much."

"How much did it charge?"

"Around one lakh rupees."

"Omg! That is insane. It is too much," Shivangi couldn't believe her ears. One lakh! She was still processing while Riya kept talking.

"Not only this, but the food was also bad. Even the water bottle was so small. There were few fruits too, but I was scared to eat anything due to the virus. How was I supposed to open my mask and have food? So, I didn't eat anything throughout my journey."

"That would have been so tough. Riya, you know, one of my friends, Tamanna, lives in the US too. She said the same thing. She didn't eat for around six hours straight after landing. She was complaining the same as you that her journey was the worst."

"The truth is no one had a smooth experience during the pandemic. Most students studying overseas had the same troubles," Riya could relate. "And in this situation, the pharma-medical companies are making a profit by selling oximeters, masks, sanitisers, and required things at a high price. No one is thinking about the country, and a few NGOs trying to help are working on a small scale. They don't have enough money."

"This is the harsh truth, Riya. These companies and big organizations don't care about people's lives. In our country, the state is inefficient in providing enough oxygen cylinders because of the high population with inadequate facilities. There are a lot of stories about people stealing oxygen cylinders to sell them at a high price. Medicines are being stolen from hospitals and later sold at double prices. This is what is happening."

"This is very sad. People are dying, losing their loved ones, and still, the evils of the society keep harming others. You know, I believe in karma, and it will take care of them," Riya sounded intense.

"Riya, but we don't know about karma yet. People are losing in the present. It doesn't matter if they get the punishment for their deeds in the future. The whole point is things are getting worse due to that."

"I understand, but it is my philosophy. I know people who recovered from Covid but did not donate plasma to the needy, and a lot of people are backing off when it comes to helping other people."

"It is the time to take care of yourself the most. People are most concerned about their families. No one is obliged to do something for someone unless it is very urgent. It is because everyone is scared to help others. Most people have become selfish. A few days ago, I read in the newspaper that a Covid patient was admitted to a hospital, and one night someone came and stole the oxygen cylinder provided to them. Then, in the morning, that patient died. It was recorded in CCTV footage," Shivangi sadly explained the article.

"Omg. Who did this and why?"

"We don't know yet. Maybe someone took it for their loved ones. It is such a shame for someone to do so."

"This is disgusting."

"Not only this, but the robbery during this time has also increased too. Considering that majority of the population is unemployed now. Their helplessness has led them to commit these crimes," Shivangi continued.

"This is wrong. Taking advantage by degrading someone in this situation is equal to a crime," Riya said.

"The prices are doubled up in the RTPCR tests. Everyone is playing a business game now."

"I realise all this is happening when the whole world is suffering. Instead of uniting, there is an increase in the crime rates."

"Yes. And not only normal citizens, but I have seen the traffic police asking for a fine for not wearing a mask in the car. You know, initially, they once stopped us. Ayaansh wasn't wearing a mask as he was eating. I was driving, I had a mask on, yet the traffic police officer stopped us and asked for one thousand rupees as a fine. I barely had three hundred rupees cash with me, and I had to use it for my blood test. They started to blackmail us when we denied paying. They took our pictures and warned us that they would upload pictures and videos of us rebelling against them on social media. They said it would go viral and defame us. I mean, are the government officers supposed to do this? That also for not wearing a mask in the car."

"Oh, that's bad. I heard a lot of stories about these traffic police officers asking for a fine from the people not wearing masks."

"Yes, they are charging so high."

"Then, what happened?"

"We somehow convinced him and requested him to let us go as we didn't have enough cash. Ayaansh was annoyed. They ask for any random amount."

"They are earning by looking at people's situation."

"Exactly. I had to go for my blood test. There would have been a problem for me if I had paid the remaining cash. Because of such incidents, I am more scared. Whenever I see traffic police, I immediately put up my mask, even in the car. Even though I have seen traffic police officers not wearing masks themselves lately. Hypocrites!" Shivangi sounded irritated. Riya nodded.

Shivangi continued, "Once, I was stopped by a group of traffic officers. They asked for my driving license, and I immediately provided them. Then they asked for PUC, and I showed that too. I was even wearing the seat belt. Finally, they let me go. After coming home, I said this to my parents, and they jokingly said that only the RC book was left. I should have shown that too," she laughed. "It might be because I am a female driver. They doubted if I didn't have my driving license."

"Well, maybe, but times are changing," Riya said.

"Yeah, okay, if you say so. Though in the modern world, women still are suppressed," Shivangi said in a softer tone wanting Riya to see the reality of the world. "It is true everywhere in the world. Here in India, there were a lot of cases of domestic violence. I watched a video of a woman sharing her experience as her husband used to hit her. During the time of lockdown, many men took advantage of isolation. No one in her society could come to help and rescue her as everyone was too scared to step out," she added.

"These monsters are taking advantage of this situation. Sometimes I wonder, where are we heading? How have we humans changed? How our lives have been affected with time. I keep asking these questions to myself. So many sad stories around the globe, the stories of people losing their lives, loved ones, their family, money, financial support, and even their dreams!" Riya said seriously.

"Yes, a lot of people have lost will and optimism too. I remember, recently I read the newspaper. There was an article about a woman who committed suicide after her husband died due to this virus. She also took her child's life. I was so disturbed by that news," Shivangi said.

"People are getting weaker. But this is the reality. We have to face it," Riya replied philosophically.

"Ugh, exactly, I am tired of coming to terms with this life."

"Though, we are all still holding up."

"But how can someone look at the bright and positive side among all the wrong that is happening."

"There are some good people who are helping others too. One of my father's friends expired a few days ago. The reason was that he was always on his feet to help anyone in his circle, even strangers. Someone in his relative was pregnant, and after delivery, she had complications at this time of the pandemic, and she was hospitalised. When he came to know. He rushed to the hospital to help her," Riya said in a sad tone.

"Seriously?"

"Yes, in the civil hospital. There were around two hundred ambulances. There are a lot of chances of getting contaminated. He even helped in taking two Covid positive patients to the hospital on his bike. He didn't even care to wear a mask. He only carried a handkerchief to cover his face. He didn't take care of himself at all," she said painfully. "Now that he is dead, it is tough for his family. He was the sole bread earner of his family. They don't have any financial support anymore."

"It is very a sad phase for all of us; for the whole world."

"Yes," Riya agreed thoroughly.

"Anyways, how were the things in the US?" Shivangi changed the topic to distract Riya.

"In the US, no one believes in savings. They only spend. There, even middle class who have money had to stand in queue for free food."

"Because they don't save?

"Yes," Riya said in an obvious tone as she added. "They think that the government shouldn't force their citizens to wear masks. People even protested against wearing masks."

"I don't understand these people. Don't they know it is a global pandemic?"

"Exactly. You know, in Sweden, they never had lockdown, but they still followed proper protocol. There was no need for lockdown.

They were disciplined enough. Not more than fifty people gathered in a single area. The death rates weren't much," Riya said.

"That is remarkable, but we can't compare every country to Sweden. Every country had its way of dealing."

"Anyways, one more thing that bothers me is that in the US, the rent is too high. The landlords are dependent on tenants, it is their income, but tenants are unemployed on their own," she added.

"Oh my God; that makes it worse."

"I know, right? One of the tenants I know got a mail from his renter to pay as fast as possible. Unfortunately, he had lost his job in the pandemic and had his whole family to feed. So, the landlord gave him three months extra to complete his overdue payment. It was a good gesture, but not everyone is like him. Many people were homeless because they didn't have any savings. If they had savings, their life would have been better."

"Yes, you are right. So how did you manage these three months in the US?"

"I have been living in the hostel for three months all alone. All my friends and roommates had already left. There was no internship for three months. It was tough."

"Oh, that is a bummer for sure. I heard you had to live with some strangers?"

"Yes, but how did you know?"

"As my dad works at the airport. Your family had called him, and then mom told me about this. She talked with your mom. She was worried for you."

"Oh. Yes, my parents were trying to be very strong for me, but you know they are parents. They will always be worried for their child."

"So why did you have to live with strangers? That is the one thing mom didn't tell me," Shivangi laughed.

"Yes, Yes, I'll tell you," Riya laughed too, "I had to shift from my hostel after my college was closed. I then lived with someone my family friend knew."

"It would have been very awkward."

"Yes, it was uncomfortable and awkward."

"But why didn't you work a part-time job while you were stuck?"

"You cannot work on a student visa, so I couldn't."

"If that is so, you were screwed."

"I told you, I was."

"And the worst part was. I got Covid."

"Really?"

"Yes. I had Covid in February this year. It was difficult for me. I was so weak and helpless, but I couldn't share my pain with anyone as I lived with strangers. The best part is they let me stay even though I had Covid. I stayed quarantined in one of their rooms. They took care of me. Provided me food and treatment. Yes, I did pay for everything, but I am grateful for them. I don't know what I would have done if I didn't find them. I mean nowhere to stay and contaminated with a virus that was killing millions all over the world," Riya said, her eyes filled with unshed tears. She didn't want to cry in front of anyone. But as she remembered that time of her life, she felt helpless. She was glad that she was with her family now. She carefully wiped away her tears, thinking that Shivangi wouldn't notice, but she did. Shivangi felt sad for her friend. She knew it was hard for her to talk about this, so she swiftly switched the topic.

"How did you get contaminated?" she asked softly. And the next instance, rage took over Riya's moist eyes.

"I think it came from our teammate. We all had to sign a declaration form, he did too, but he wasn't feeling good. Then it turned out he had the virus. After a day, I wasn't feeling well, so I got tested, and it was positive. I am damn sure it was him. I still curse him," Riya spat. Her pain, agony, and anger were clearly visible.

"Hey, it's okay, Riya. I know I can't understand what you had to go through. But you are fine now, and that's such a great thing."

"I know, but still, how can he be so careless? Because of him, everyone in our team got contaminated. He shouldn't have lied on the declaration form," Riya said in aggression.

"I don't think he did it deliberately. It was a new experience for every one of us. We were terrified and unaware of everything. Maybe he didn't know," Shivangi sighed. "Past is past, Riya. Let it go."

"Yes, I have to. But when I was in isolation, it was too much for me. I was so bored. I needed a break from being in one place. It was monotonous; I was mentally exhausted. I had nothing to do. I felt like I was trapped in jail. I did have my phone and laptop, I watched movies and shows, but the loss of freedom was hindering my mental state. The day I recovered, all I did was stand by the open window and breathe fresh air. And when dad told me that my ticket was booked and I was coming back, I was so happy that I broke down on the call itself. My mom and dad were worried about what had happened, but when I told them I was happy, they got relaxed, but I think they both cried a few tears too," Riya chuckled.

"I am so glad you are finally home with your family and completely fit and fine."

"Yes, me too. These four months have made me think about so much. About how there is so much bad in the world but at the same time, there is good too. And you know one thing? It's both sad and funny- nowadays, if someone sneezes, everyone is scared that it might be coronavirus. Earlier, my friends used to say, 'God bless you,' Now, they say, 'Oh my God!'" she laughed.

"Yes, that is true," Shivangi laughed too.

Shivangi looked back on their conversation. She couldn't help but ask one question that was disturbing her.

"Well, where are we heading?" Shivangi asked and sighed.

"I don't think anyone knows the answer," Riya shrugged.

6

THE COMFORT ZONES OF OUR OWN

"I remember the days when I was traveling and playing tennis at the beginning of last year, and of course, that feeling when I won the medal. I cherish those moments, and sometimes I wonder if these moments are ever going to come back?" Shivangi asked Samaira while they were sitting at Shivangi's house. She asked the same question during their daily round of video calls. She couldn't help but bring up the same question again and again.

"Of course, you will be able to live those moments again. Just have patience. We all are going through the same fear, but I am hopeful," Samaira said, trying to comfort Shivangi as always. Her answer was the same every day that Shivangi had memorised these lines.

"You keep saying the same thing every day," Shivangi said in a troubled voice.

"Because you ask the same question every day," Samaira shrugged. She knew Shivangi was upset, but she wanted to stay optimistic, and she kept motivating her friends too.

"Yes, I know, but I am not used to staying at home. Even you are not. Right?" Shivangi questioned, but before Samaira could answer, she continued. "At the beginning of the lockdown, I was more productive, and now I am procrastinating a lot. Not able to sit for long and study. My sleep schedule is messed up; I am not waking up early in the morning. The only constant thing is my workout schedule. At least, I am habitual to that."

"I understand. See, though I am not habitual to staying at home, I have been comfortable lately. I am still an introvert. I realised I like staying at home to spend some time with myself," Samaira said.

"That is so you, Samu. You always enjoy your own company anyways. I was wondering if I had forgotten how to drive a car or to even hold the tennis racquet, but I got a chance to drive again, and I realised I got better control from the break. But I am pretty sure I might take some time to get my game back," Shivangi said as her mother bought coffee for them.

"Sometimes, a break can improve your skills. I am glad we are safe and are having a good time at our homes, while many of my friends are stuck away from their homes. I know the feeling of finally coming back home. I have realised the value of my family and loved ones," Samaira said, not making eye contact and shrugging. Serious conversations with friends always made her a little shy. She didn't want to sound philosophical but rather casual.

Shivangi understood her friend's dilemma and wanted to lighten the mood. She took a sip of her coffee and asked, "I am included in the loved ones, right?"

"No, you are not," Samaira joked back.

"You need to work on your sarcasm," Shivangi smirked.

"Ha-ha, very funny," Samaira mocked.

Their friendship of more than fifteen years has always blossomed and grew stronger through the years. These friendly banters were very common among them.

"Samu, don't you think this pandemic has taught us to be happy for the small things? There's the realization that only materialistic things are not the most important thing in our lives. Finally, I have got this chance to sit at my home and relax. The whole world has taken a break," Shivangi said as she took another sip of her coffee.

"Yes, that is so true. This time has taught us that we can work from our homes. We can cook amazing delicacies with the least available things from the market. I have become more independent during this quarantine. I have become a better version of myself," Samaira sipped her coffee too.

"Same here, Samu. I have discovered a lot of things about myself. It has been mentally exhausting for me as we all are isolated. But we can still enjoy under the shelter of our homes," Shivangi smiled.

Suddenly Shivangi remembered her conversation with Tamanna a few months ago when she had come to India.

***

May 2020

Tamanna had come back from the US a day before the lockdown started. But she hadn't left the house since.

"You know, I didn't eat for six hours straight when I was at the airport," Tamanna said. Shivangi had called Tamanna as soon as she heard that she had come back from the US. She was her family friend. They had known each other for a long time as they used to play tennis together.

"How come?" Shivangi asked astonishingly.

"My flight was fourteen hours long from Chicago to Delhi and then a connecting flight from Delhi to Ahmedabad. I had to wait for the second flight from Delhi to Ahmedabad. It was too crowded. Everyone was wearing their masks. I was so scared to remove it and eat anything. I was worried as there was no distance maintained between the public, so I didn't want to take the risk of eating or drinking."

"That is so sad, but the feeling of finally coming back home must have been so amazing."

"It indeed was. Honestly, I was too grateful for my life at that moment. At least, my parents could provide me with the resources to come back home. Now, I am more patient. I still remember, at one point, I was at the airport, and I almost fainted, but thankfully there was an aunty. She helped me throughout the long journey."

"It is good to have some company, especially during this kind of hectic journey," Shivangi said.

"Yes. But that was not the worst part. After I came home, lockdown happened. I had to stay isolated at my home, which messed up my mental health."

"Why? What happened?"

"I was missing the time when I was occupied with my work, meeting friends and everything. I didn't even feel like working out, so I gained weight. I ate a lot, I had sugar cravings, and I watched a lot of series. I was being lethargic. I was so anxious that I felt annoyed with every single thing. I would freak out over anything," Tamanna finally sighed after she said everything in one go.

It felt like she kept all these things hidden in her heart and hadn't spoken about them to anyone. Shivangi was like a therapist to all her friends. Everyone would pour their worries and problems to her, and Tamanna did the same.

"I remember one day when mom made lunch, she forgot to add salt. When I took the first bite, I was terrified that I had lost my sense of taste. I jumped up from my seat and ran to my room and shut myself. When mom asked me what happened, I said nothing. She got so worried. She felt something was wrong, so when she tasted the food, she remembered that she might have forgotten to add salt. When she told me, I confirmed with her twice before I opened the door and hugged her. I was so relieved," Tamanna said without pausing for a breath. She sighed as if she, let go of the burden of that memory.

Shivangi could not say anything. She simply sat there, holding her phone to her ear, and let Tamanna speak.

"You know, the only thing which made me happier is meeting my cousins. Mom and I have come to live with them for a month at their house. We were bored, all alone in such a spacious house. We had nothing to do. So, we decided and somehow managed to come here,"

Tamanna said. Her father was in another city, so she and her mom were alone in the large house.

"Oh, so you are at your uncle's place now. That is great," Shivangi said. "You did the right thing. It must have been so hard for you to be isolated all alone. At least spending time with your cousins keeps you occupied, and you can actually enjoy rather than sitting at one place and doing nothing."

"Yes, on that day, mom decided that we were going to come here, to my uncle's house. That is why I am happy now. Even though I am still stressed a little but living with them is helping me. Sometimes I think that home is where everyone should feel calm. Unfortunately, it was the opposite for me. I felt so disturbed. I feel I should have never come back. My life in the US was so good. I was busy and happy," Tamanna said with a sad smile.

Even though Shivangi said, "I understand, Tamanna," she was still trying to understand Tamanna's point of view.

Shivangi had a very different point of view on the whole situation. She was happy that she was at her house, safe and secure, with her family. She sometimes missed her tennis sessions and felt worried about her future. She missed hanging out with her friends too. But currently, she was satisfied that she, her family, her friends, everyone were safe at their homes. She considered herself lucky to be in the comfort of her home. But as she thought further, she understood that every person has a different comfort place. For Shivangi, it was her house; for Samaira, it was equally her house and her hostel, and the same way for Tamanna, it was in the US with her work and friends.

"So, what do you guys do?" Shivangi asked, coming out of her thoughts.

"We play board games together, sometimes even cards. I have learned so many new cards games in two days only. It is really fun," Tamanna smiled.

"Oh, board games are fun. Even my full family sits down every night and plays board games. Sometimes we play cards and carom. We play a new game every day. So, we won't get bored," Shivangi said. She was about to mention after every game, she and her father worked out. But then remembered how Tamanna was coping with her workout schedule, so she didn't say anything.

"Yes, now that I have gone through a lot, I have developed a good coping mechanism in life. I am now more hopeful towards life, I would say."

"Really? What exactly changed you, Tamanna?" Shivangi chuckled.

"You know, I used social media a lot, so I desperately needed a break from it. I am now trying to do other stuff like painting. I have now started to meditate, too. I have learned whatever time you spend with your family; you should be grateful for that. I have grown gratitude towards my life."

"Tamanna, this is an amazing transformation. I assume all this happened after your journey of ups and downs in this pandemic?"

"Definitely. That is what has changed me. I learned living in the present as life is unpredictable. No one knows, what will happen next year, so being here in the moment is important."

"This is a huge change, Tamanna," Shivangi was awestruck.

"I grew up from a lot of things. You should hear my favourite quote. I have learned this by heart, 'When things feel overwhelming, remember, one thought at a time, one task at a time and one day at a time,' I keep telling this to myself."

"Wow, it is so well said. It has become my favourite quote too," Shivangi smiled.

***

Present

"Shivangi, Shivangi!" she came out of her thoughts as Samaira called her out and asked, "Where are you lost?"

"Nothing. What were you saying?" she asked.

Samaira let it go. She knew that Shivangi would always think deeply about everything she saw or heard and was sure that something from the conversation had triggered her memory.

She calmly repeated herself, "I was saying we both are in the comfort zones of our home."

"Own," Shivangi mumbled to correct Samaira. When Samaira asked what she meant, she shook her head, and Samaira let it go too. They had already talked for hours, and Samaira had to go and study. So, she bid bye to Shivangi and her family and went home.

As soon as Samaira left, Shivangi fell into deep thought. She felt so grateful and happy about her life. She thought about the blessings she had, and when she was zoned out in her own thoughts, Ayaansh came in to call her for dinner. She turned to him and flashed a huge smile that creeped out Ayaansh.

"What is wrong?" he asked as he looked around. "Why are you smiling like the joker?"

The next moment she took him in a hug. He was shocked at first, then confused and suspicious. Instead of hugging her back, he started pushing himself out of the hug shouting for his mom, "Mom, something has happened to *di*."

And when finally, she let him go, he ran back to the dining room and sat in his chair, giving weird looks to Shivangi, who followed him. Shivangi then went to hug her mom, dad, and *Dadi* (grandma), and everyone was as surprised as Ayaansh was. But her dad, mom, *Dadi* hugged her back, and she sat down in her chair with a happy smile on her face.

"What happened to you all of a sudden?" her mom asked the question that was running through everyone's mind.

"I realised something," she said gleefully.

"I see. What did you realise, *beta*?"

"This pandemic taught us to be happy for the small things," she replied.

The elders exchanged looks, and Ayaansh kept staring at her while she set up her plate. When she heard nothing for the next minute, except for the buzzing silence and the clattering of her plate and spoons, she looked up at everyone, which brought everyone out of their reverie. They all served their plates and sat down to eat. The silence was finally broken by her mom.

"Remember when I used to rush to take you for your tennis sessions, packing your tiffin as fast as possible, waking up early in the morning. There was no time to rest; it was all work. Now, we are finally relaxed. We have time for our family and friends, and even in this deadly pandemic, we are smiling every day," her mother said as she took the first bite.

Shivangi and all the others nodded, and there was no exchange of the words for the whole dinner, but all faces were lit with a tiny smile.

Shivangi found herself in a relaxed state, happy to be around her family. She has grown, learned, and achieved in the comfort of her own house. *Home sweet home*, she thought and smiled.

7

THE BLAME GAME

Whether it is day or night, everything looks the same. I cannot differentiate which day is today as every day seems to be Sunday, thought Shivangi as she woke up late in the morning. There was nothing new to hear. The same ranting of the news channels about the increasing cases and the repetitive cycle of public blaming the administration. Who is responsible, anyways? She had barely opened her eyes when she heard her father and grandma discussing the current situation.

As Shivangi walked out of the room, she saw her father talking to his brothers on a video call. She could hear both of her uncles. Sanjay had two younger brothers. Mr. Ronish was the second brother who lived in Gurgaon, and Mr. Sakash was the youngest, a software engineer in the US. *Ronish uncle and papa's thoughts never match. On the other hand, Sakash uncle always agrees with papa, but only because he loves boasting about his country and shaming our country,* Shivangi thought.

"The thing is, there was so much chaos here, especially in March, April, and May. A lot of people died, as everyone was figuring out back then, and we didn't have much knowledge. Also, the doctors weren't prepared for such a sudden outburst. The US was hit before other countries. The first-hand experience came from the US, Italy, Germany, Brazil, and a few other countries," Sakash was as usual bragging about the country he resided in. "But now we are doing so much better. I can't say the same for India."

"If it keeps going like this, then nothing is going to change in this country. Our government is hardly doing anything for us. All this chaos and deaths in huge numbers. It is the government's fault. It is their responsibility to take care of it," her father said.

The TV was switched on in the background. Her grandma was sitting quietly and agreeing to whatever Sanjay said. A lot of people were blaming the government for not being able to handle the situation effectively and for taking advantage of people's helplessness. However, her uncle didn't seem to agree.

"See, it is not exactly like that, b*haiya* (brother). Okay, some of the people that work in my office are from other countries. We got in contact because of the work from home. Even they keep blaming their government. But the public should be more aware, to take care of themselves. You cannot completely blame the government. Look at the people around. I have seen a lot of people not following Covid protocols. No one is serious about social distancing. Yesterday when I went shopping, I saw people standing so close in a queue. No one cared about maintaining a distance. What can the government do in this?" Ronish said.

"But not everything is in the public's hand, and if no one is happy with their government, the government could be wrong," Sakash mumbled and then added. "See, now it is more infectious, even if you are six feet apart, and you have the chance to get contaminated by the virus. Mask isn't enough this time. They think they can be protected by this distance, but it was useful in the first wave, not in the second one. The government has to do more than making circles," he mocked.

"Public does what they are told. The government is supposed to be stricter during these times," her father added.

"It won't help. The public will do what they want to. Aren't they scared of the second wave?" Ronish asked.

The fear of the second wave had started. Shivangi was so done with all this. Every day they hoped it would get better after the first wave had settled. But there were already talks about the second wave. Other counties were already hit with the second wave.

"Even if they are, what can they do? Look at the population. Here we keep getting updates about our country. People are laughing at us. The way they are handling the situation is ridiculous," Sakash seemed to be frustrated with the country even though he was not even living there. Sanjay somewhere disagreed, but he ignored his younger brother's comment.

"The government can take action, form proper rules, why won't people follow? And, of course, people are scared. Here, no one is stepping out of the house, despite there being no lockdown," her father said now a little calmly.

"Anyways, look at the system. It is collapsing. People are blaming each other. Politics is used in the wrong way. Businesses have no more profits. We all are screwed," Sakash said. It seemed to Shivangi that all Sakash wanted to do, was start arguments. "But that's only for India. Here in the US, offices have opened."

"You are allowed to enter the office during these times?" Shivangi joined the conversation and asked, intrigued.

"Yes, but we need to sign a declaration form online, then only you are allowed to enter."

"How do they know if you have signed or not?"

"It is automated. It shows if the person has signed or not. In this second wave, you need to work remotely until seven of September, and after that, we might be able to go back to the office, but we still need to sign a declaration form every day," Sakash boasted as he added. "But I don't think you guys should open offices. Your government should make better decisions."

"I don't think so, *bhaiya*. People are careless nowadays. The first wave had people on their toes. This time people are dying, yet they are not serious about the situation. My neighbour had gone on a vacation with his family a few days ago, and now they are quarantined. His wife is sick, and now they are in a panic if they have had contaminated this virus. What role does the government play in this?" Ronish was now very upset with both of his brothers.

"I agree it was their mistake, but there are only a few people like that," Sanjay argued.

"It is not about that. Some people have lost their family members. They blame the government but still keep repeating the same mistakes. The government cannot be changed immediately. People have to be more sensible."

"You seem like a blindfolded person. I don't want to talk to you about that now," Sanjay got a little disappointed.

"The government there is doing a criminal act, knowing the consequences, yet it doesn't affect them. Here, the situation is different. Every Indian here is worried about the actions taken by the Indian government," Sakash added.

"Fine, we can stop, but you have to respect my opinion. The truth is we all are blaming each other during this pandemic. Some are blaming nature, some are blaming God, and some are blaming themselves for their karma. So, we cannot assume and focus on anyone's mistake," Ronish tried to explain extensively.

Shivangi agreed with her uncle but didn't say a word to her dad. Sanjay got up, handed the phone to Shivangi, and left. She smiled apologetically at her uncle. Sakash also bid a very hurried bye and cut the call. Now it was only Shivangi and Ronish. She relaxed and greeted him with a smile.

"*Chachu*, you are right about nature. While we all were at our respective homes, the environment had finally gotten a break from us. It was free from the harmful effects we humans have made."

"There is no major improvement in the environment, but there was some good news like ozone layer had filled itself, because it didn't have disturbance from us. I would consider it the best news so far. In the past few years, I have only heard about the global warming, melting of the glaciers, the pollution, the hole in the ozone layer, and whatnot," Ronish said seriously. He removed his specs, rubbed his eyes, and then wore it again. They were looking too large.

"*Chachu*, did you change your spectacles?"

"Yes, my number has increased as I am sitting on my laptop every day. There is no way I am going to my office. It is work from home only. But this working from home is taking the hell out of me," he said, a little frustrated.

"I can understand. It must have been tough. I realised that the virus is not attacking a particular religion. Everyone has been affected badly. The irony is that humans are coming together. There is no discrimination of caste or religious beliefs. We are blaming each other and yet supporting each other, which shows humanity is the biggest religion in the world."

"Well, this is a deep thought, Shivangi. How do you come up with this? You are right. The virus spreads and doesn't differentiate between religion, caste, or if you are poor or rich. The public is blaming the doctors and hitting them. Didn't you hear, there have been many attacks in the public hospitals in Delhi? The violence can lead to a major loss of the general public if the medical staffs start to riot."

"Yes, there is absolutely no point of doing that. But I am confused about who is responsible for all the mess created in the pandemic? Is it the fault of the country from where it all started?"

"We don't know who is responsible. Blaming a particular country like this is not the right thing. Even though we know from where the virus started, it's better to focus on the future. The only solution is to come and fight together. You don't have to worry. Things will be alright."

"You are right, but I am frustrated."

"We all are at some level, but these things are not in our hands, except taking care of ourselves. There is a famous theory by Malthus that says there are three factors that control the human population when it exceeds the earth's capacity. The three factors are war, famine, and disease. We can say according to this theory that nature acts upon itself if things go out of its limited capacity."

"Which theory is this, *Chachu*?" Shivangi found it a very interesting way to describe the situation.

"This is an economic theory on population. But can we give back and let nature heal itself? Or were we just created to take from it? Can we compromise our routines and lifestyle? The truth is, we can't," he explained.

"I agree, *Chachu*," Shivangi nodded.

"This can be an eye-opener for all of us to realise that even if we go back to our normal routine, we should think about the harm we are doing to nature, and then we might be able to move on from the disasters."

"I cannot see that happening anyways. We will still keep doing everything we have been doing and point fingers at each other," Shivangi shook her head in disappointment.

He smiled and said, "This is the truth, beta. You have understood a lot of deeper things in life. I am glad you are growing and learning about everything happening in and around your life. For now, I need to go. There is a meeting scheduled. Just let *bhaiya* know that blaming the government isn't going to help."

Shivangi was keen to observe everything they were talking about. She couldn't take one side, but she kept wondering, when will this blame game end? As he bid goodbye to her, she smiled and looked at her dad sitting in front of her, listening to the whole conversation the whole time. She stood up and went to brush her teeth and start her day.

8

THE REALITY

It was a silent afternoon except for Ayaansh screaming, "Yes!" and, "No, you are stupid," as he played on his computer. Shivangi's mom and grandma were taking their usual nap, and her dad was at work. She took her diary and pen, ran out to the Veranda, and sat down to continue her journal of life. She was writing everything she observed around her during the pandemic. In this despair, she found that writing gave her hope.

Shivangi had a habit of going through her old notes before she would add anything new. As she read through her notes, she found something that triggered her memory and made her feel how far they have come.

***

May 2020

With the knowledge of privilege, Shivangi even understood the irony of nature. During the lockdown, humans experienced the meaning of being in a cage without freedom. They felt the pain of animals and the life they live. She remembered the news about elephants coming out on the road. The wild animals stepped out while humans watched them from inside their homes, roaming free on man-made roads. Shivangi felt like nature was healing and taking a break from humans.

After a whole one and half months of staying at home, Shivangi got out of the house with her mother and grandma. They were driving for her grandma's dental treatment. The clinic was open only because it was the orange zone, and it was open only for consultation or emergency procedures.

"Thank God we are going out of this house. I have got a headache staying at home all the time," Shivangi said excitedly.

"Only because it's important, otherwise you know how bad the situation is, and we should not be going out at all," Amita said strictly. Shivangi nodded as she sat in the passenger seat, and Amita took the driver's seat. Her grandma sat at the back and fell asleep as soon as they started driving.

They wore masks even in the car. Once out on the road, Shivangi couldn't believe her eyes. Everything was so different. The roads were empty, and it felt like they had been abandoned. As if no person had set foot on them for years. Every single shop was closed except a few grocery and medical stores. Even they had to follow specific rules.

"Mom, there is no one I can see, not even a single person on the streets," Shivangi spoke.

"Mhm Hm," nodded Amita as she took a turn, and Shivangi spotted a young boy on the footpath. Wearing a tore off white vest with khaki pants. He was barefoot. She could see his mesmerizing eyes filled with sadness, hunger, and then hope when he spotted the car. He ran towards them. It was visible that he had not eaten in a while. Her mother pulled the car over and thought of giving him money, but then Shivangi spoke, "Mom, what will he do with the money? There is no shop open to food. Shall we give him half the lunch we packed for Dr Ayush?" she asked.

Amita agreed and split the food in half and packed it in an extra foil they had. But before opening the window, she wore gloves and checked if she was wearing the mask. As soon as she placed the packet in the boy's hand, he started sobbing, folding his hands, and thanking them in his welled-up voice. He ran to the footpath and quickly tore open the foil and didn't wait another second to eat. As soon as he took the first bite, he broke down. Shivangi and her mom were still there watching him with so much pain and pity. After watching this, Shivangi's eyes filled with tears, and before she would break down too, Amita drove off.

The weather was burning hot. As they drove, they could see a lot of police officers in every corner, standing under the sun and sweating out. Their duty was to make sure no one stepped out of the house. Shivangi and Amita saluted them from the car, which bought a smile on their faces.

Shivangi was in deep thought for the rest of the drive. Once they reached the clinic, they greeted Dr Ayush and handed him lunch. His clinic was shut for two weeks as his family and staff were contaminated. His family had just recovered, so Amita thought to carry some lunch for him. Even though he refused, they insisted, so he had to take it.

"Actually, we all were contaminated with the coronavirus. So, we had to close the clinic for a few days. We couldn't take any risks with the patients," Dr Ayush said calmly.

"Of course, how are you and your family now?" Amita asked in condolement.

"We all are good, considering I already had antibodies by working in this environment. As you know, my wife is in the same field, so she is fine too. My children have good immunity as well. So, we all recovered well enough."

"Oh, it's great to hear."

Shivangi's grandma was having her check-up done. The procedure was going on, and they had to wait for a while. Shivangi was very intrigued and wanted to ask Dr Ayush a few questions. She started in a soft tone, "Doctor, how has your experience been?"

"*Beta*, the number of deaths we've faced this year is much more than last so many years. From senior citizens to the younger ones who are the sole bread earner have lost their lives. It is so emotional and devastating at the same time. It has disturbed me to the core," Dr Ayush answered.

"I can feel it too, doctor. Everyone is feeling low mentally," she said.

"I mean, psychologically, I am totally fine. I am stable when it comes to my mental health. Maybe because I haven't lost anyone closer in my life, and I am thankful for that."

"It's good to hear, doctor. I think you are very busy. Many patients are coming for the dental treatment," said Amita.

"Exactly, and that is why I am doing fine mentally. I am busy in my professional life but look at other people like small shop owners, vegetable vendors, and small business owners. They are all in a very bad position. I am busy in my life. So, whatever is happening outside in the world isn't affecting me much, but those people sitting at their homes with nothing to do, keep thinking about the situation. They keep overthinking. It is like the idiom, 'An idle mind is the devil's workshop,'" Dr Ayush said.

"Yes, doctor, how has your journey been in this pandemic?" Shivangi asked reluctantly. She didn't want to agitate him with a bundle of questions. But she couldn't keep her curiosity at bay.

Dr Ayush smiled. He was, in turn, very happy to talk about it. For the last few months, all he had was sad exchanges with patients and their families. So, he was very happy to have a decent conversation, "Well, as you know, I am a dental surgeon. So, I had never been to a ward before. I had never seen a dead body before. But now, I have seen it. I did those things that I had never done in my life before as a medical professional. With this pandemic, I saw a lot, felt a lot, and experienced different things."

"Oh, do you feel different too, like a little strange about it?" she asked.

"Not exactly, but yes, it has been a pretty different year for me altogether. Though the good thing is my family is happy. They are totally fine. We are coping with it well enough. I am a little worried about my mother. She is a gynaecologist, living alone in Mysore, and is seventy-three years old. Though she is independent, working there all alone at this age, I am a little worried about her. Although, my mother keeps herself busy by checking on patients. So, it is good for her mentally and physically that she is active."

"This is true, doctor. Your mother is an inspiration. Even at this age, she is so active."

"Yes, I just wish her to be safe."

They all smiled. Dr Ayush then stood up and went in for the further procedure. Shivangi understood one important thing from the conversation- the importance of being occupied in life. Sometimes the work you do keeps you away from all the stress.

The whole ride back home, Shivangi kept thinking about the two worlds. One where she lived, safe and happy inside her house, and one where people were suffering and striving to have even one bite of food or helping others by putting their own life at risk. It was like she got a reality check about the outer world.

***

Present

Not able to handle so many emotions, she decided to do the one thing that always calms her. She started writing her thoughts.

She wrote about the two worlds she had got to know. She wrote about reality.

"Dear diary," Read Shivangi, as she had the habit of reading out loud as she wrote.

"I saw a new world. While everyone hopes that everything goes back to normal, we have no idea what this pandemic has brought for us. The cases are at peak. We are sitting at our homes, cleaning, doing things we never did. As for me, I cooked. Yes, yes. I cooked. Of course, mom was guiding me, and Ayaansh made fun of my food even though dad and *Dadi* said it was yummy. We are bonding so much. Dad and I work out daily, and as you know, Ayaansh is a lazy boy. He does nothing but plays on his computer...."

"Yes! I told you, we will win this game," Ayaansh shouted, which startled everyone. Before Shivangi could scream at him, she heard her mother's room door open, and she chuckled. He was going to get an earful. She shook her head and went back to her diary.

"...play on his computer. Mom keeps making these amazing dishes. We bake so many new things. But she also asks us to drink and eat healthy for immunity, and she's not wrong. I am sure it will always be a memorable year for our lifetime. But for others?" Shivangi paused and looked up from her diary. She remembered everything she had seen and heard from the news, her friends, and that day with her own eyes.

"I had to sneak in because everyone was scared of people that travelled altogether from a different country. I had to lie to the security guard that I was in India only," Tamanna had said. She was afraid that people from her colony wouldn't understand her condition.

"But it is all about games. He keeps playing and making videos. The truth is, he is all alone in the lockdown, and he has no siblings and friends to play with. At least I have my brother with me, we can pass the time, but he has no one," Riya had mentioned when she was talking about her 12-year-old cousin. Shivangi understood what she meant. She had a cousin sister Myra who was still a kid. Myra was a single child, and she would daily call and talk to Ayaansh and her. She would say, "*Didi*, I miss going out and playing. Why are we staying at home for so long? Why is there no school? Mummy says we need to take leave. Before, she would not let me take a leave even when I got sick. She would say that I should go out and play and not spend time on the phone, and now she won't let me go out only."

People were suffering in ways no one would have imagined. She thought about Samaira. Unlike Shivangi, Samaira didn't get to spend so much time with her father. Samaira's father had to start work from home. And the workload, instead of falling, lifted a lot. She remembered talking with Samaira about it.

"The irony is, for some people, workload before the pandemic was higher, but for others, the workload increased tremendously after this pandemic stroked us all. The concept of work from home is hyped right now. It doesn't even matter which sector or field you are in, everywhere it's the same, except a few fields like medical," Samaira had said.

Shivangi started scribbling, "Internet became the most used thing, not only for the work but to connect with people all around the world. There is so much buzz about social media. Suddenly its use and value has increased. People who never used one have joined these platforms to get out of their boring lifestyle at home. You know, one day, mom came up to me and asked me to make a profile for her Instagram. I was so shocked. I mean, I didn't have anything to hide from her, but even then, I convinced her that it was a waste of time. She finally agreed, and I was so relaxed. And don't get me started on zoom. All I have heard for one whole month was zoom, zoom, and zoom."

"Do you even know what zoom is?" she questioned her diary as if talking to a friend. Amita, who was going back to her nap after she lectured Ayaansh enough, heard her and came to check on her.

"Who are you talking to?" she asked.

"Huh!" Shivangi was startled. Her mother raised her eyebrows, to which Shivangi smiled sheepishly and gestured to her diary. Her mother shook her head in amusement and left.

Shivangi had a very good bond with her parents. After her mother left, she went back to writing.

"…It sounds like a buzzing bee flying around my ears all the time, but it's invisible. The number of people meeting on a 'Zoom meet' is more as compared to the people in a family or the neighbourhood."

As she wrote, she remembered how families stayed away from each other. She recalled a few of her friends living in a hostel. They would tell her how they felt isolated. It even led to mental health issues like anxiety, stress, and in some cases, depression, and they had to seek therapy too.

"I have started reading so many articles and blogs. I read that according to psychology—if you are isolated at a single place for a long time without a social gathering, your mental health can be affected badly because we humans are social animals. Do you know Pulu? Samaira's cat. I didn't like her before, but now, when I see that Pulu is keeping Samaira more company than anything else, I feel so happy for her. The pets are happy too. Their owners are spending time with them. It's such a joy for them."

"*Di*! Where are you?" Ayaansh screamed, and Shivangi almost threw her pen in fright. "In the veranda," she shouted back, and when he came out, she glared at him as she said, "Don't shout. Mom will lecture you again." To which he rolled his eyes.

"Did you change the Netflix password again?" Ayaansh asked, or rather, accused her with eyebrows drawn together and both hands on hips.

"No, I did not," she gave a fake smile. "But maybe Diuja did. It's her account, after all."

"I am sure you only told her to," he mumbled and went back to his room, and she smirked.

Of course, she had told Diuja to change the password. He was always messing with her wish list on Netflix, and she wanted revenge. She chuckled to herself. She took her phone and forwarded him the new password Diuja sent her. She knew she had to share it anyway. She missed watching movies in theatres with her friend, shouting and laughing. Now everyone watches what they want on their phones and laptops. She shook her head and looked up. Her eyes fell on the shop opposite their house; it was a small tea-coffee shop. She knew the uncle that worked there. She wondered how much loss the world was facing. How were these shop owners surviving? So much pain and loss. What has happened to the world? She sighed. She took her pen and rolled it between her fingers. She wanted to write everything that she was thinking, but somehow, she couldn't. She told the diary everything. But today, she felt like she didn't want to write anything that she didn't want to remember in the future.

"It seems like our magical world of dreams is very different from the reality of life. As they say, everything has its pros and cons. These years haven't been easy at all. History has proven that the pandemic occurs every hundred years. From 1720 to 2020, pandemics have threatened humanity every hundred years. The 1720 plague destroyed humankind at that time. Then cholera in 1820 killed millions of people. The Spanish flu, which occurred in 1918, was an unusually deadly influenza pandemic. It lasted till 1920, killing millions of people around the globe. Exact after hundred years, the pandemic has hit us again. There's a theory that concludes that every hundred years, a pandemic happens, which is true. However, the times have changed as well as the technology and the capacity to tackle the situations," Shivangi concluded, and without a bye, she closed the book. She had heard this theory in a video.

She kept her book in her room and spent the rest of the day teasing Ayaansh, which ended in both of them fighting which woke up their mom, and they both heard her scolding. It was almost night when her dad came back. He took a bath to keep his family safe as he had come from outside.

Before dinner, Shivangi started the conversation, "Papa, as we are born in the 21st century. We have a lot of facilities by default. We are handling this situation with easier and better communication. We can't even think about what the people in the 19th century and before that might have gone through," she said after she told her dad about the 1720 to 2020 theory.

"Absolutely, we are lucky to be able to tackle this global epidemic with better communication," he said with a smile.

Shivangi could conclude only one thing, there are people whose lives changed for good or didn't change at all, and there were people who lost time, money, and loved ones. Their time has changed forever. But we all had to face it because this is the reality.

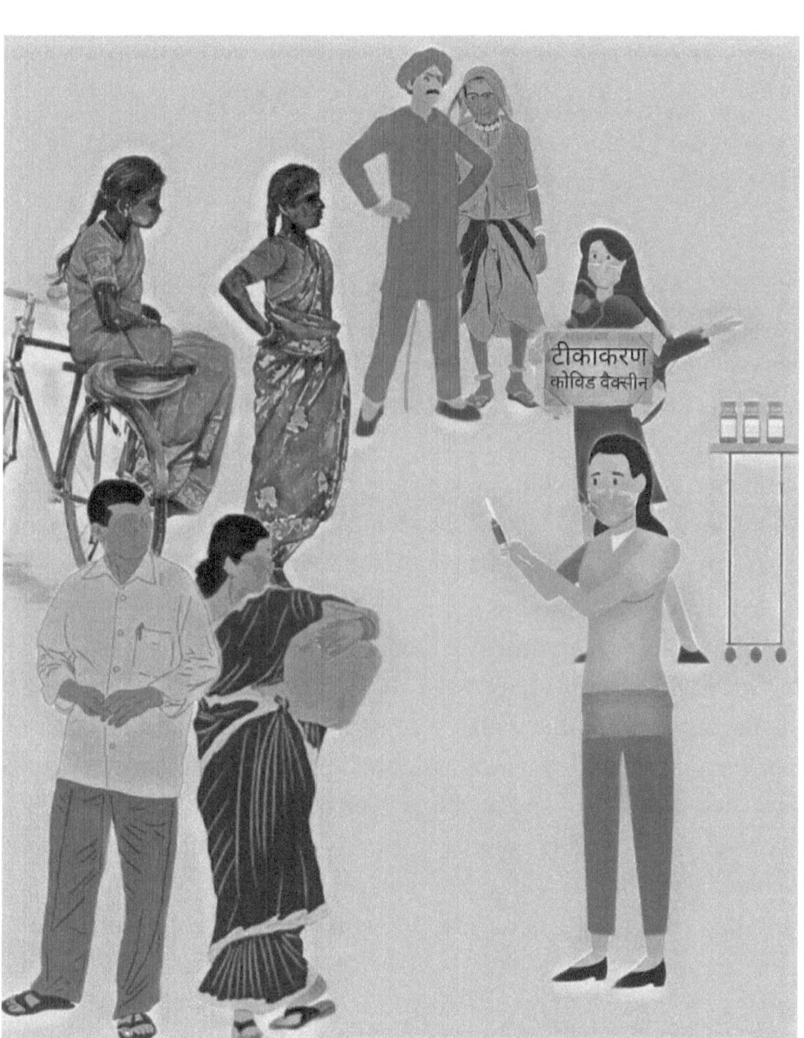
टीकाकरण
कोविड वैक्सीन

9

DOES THIS VIRUS EXIST?

The winters were here, and everything seemed to be back to normal. Shivangi had been going to her tennis sessions regularly. After everything she had heard and seen in the news, she woke up one morning to a piece of news that made her the happiest. The lockdown was unlocked in June. By mid-June, Shivangi got to know about her tennis sessions re-opening with proper guidelines and strict rules. She wasn't sure if she should step out of the house. Even if the cases weren't much, the pandemic wasn't over yet.

Ayaansh went to the same tennis sessions as Shivangi and being at home for so many months had made him insane. He kept his word that even if Shivangi didn't want to go, he would go as he missed playing tennis. Her mother agreed too, of course, after adding her list of every instruction from sanitizing their hands and not forgetting to wear their masks. Shivangi was still unsure about the whole situation. But even she missed playing tennis and stepping out of the house. Finally, when Sanjay came home, the sibling duo ran to him to complain about one another. He thought about it, and at dinner, he said, "Shivangi is right. We should wait for a little while. How about starting on the 1st of July? I know it won't magically end by then, but that doesn't mean we will stop everything and sit at our homes forever. We will let others go first and see the exact situation, then we decide. Anyways, you kids need fresh air, go to the sessions but take necessary precautions."

Shivangi understood. She readily agreed, and Ayaansh was very excited to be finally back on the court.

Shivangi had been very jubilant since she restarted her tennis sessions. She had forgotten the rush to hold the racquet in her hand, but after all these months when she held the racquet, she felt alive again. She was happy but safe as well. Both Ayaansh and Shivangi would keep sanitizing their hands every time they would step out of the house.

***

Shivangi and Diuja were talking one evening when they landed back to the topic of vacation, as always.

"We will definitely go to Goa next year," she said. They both had been planning a vacation for so long.

"Yes. For sure," Shivangi replied in optimism.

"We will enjoy everything from next year, and things are getting better now. I hope my college re-opens soon," Diuja replied in excitement. She had started planning for her offline college classes. Samaira, on the other hand, was to leave for her hostel the next month. Ayaansh was still waiting for his college admission process to start. Among everything, it was Shivangi's birthday in a few days, and she had decided to call her friends.

"That will happen soon," Shivangi said in encouragement, then added. "Ayaansh's birthday couldn't be celebrated because of the lockdown. We didn't even buy a cake. But now my birthday is coming, and we will buy a cake. I will decorate the house and call a few friends too. I am so excited for the celebration."

"Will you be calling Samaira too?" She asked in curiosity.

"Of course, why not? She lives beside me, though I wish you were here too."

"Only if we both lived in the same city. At least you have Samaira there. You guys should have fun. I hope you will miss me."

"Diuja, are you jealous?" Shivangi teased.

"No, I am not. I am simply reminding you to miss me."

"You don't need to remind me, Diu. I already miss you."

A lot of times, Diuja felt left out. She thought Shivangi and Samaira were closer, both in distance and bond. But to Shivangi, both of her friends were equally important.

"Okay. Now, go plan for your birthday."

Shivangi nodded and bid her bye.

Shivangi had invited her neighbours, Samaira, and the sibling trio Sonali, Akshara, and Kiaan. Ayaansh invited his best friend Veer as well. Surprisingly, Shivangi's parents had ordered food from outside.

Everyone was happy about finally celebrating something, but Samaira seemed off. She was wearing a surgical mask the whole time and even stood far away from everyone. She didn't even shake hands or hug Shivangi.

"Why are you standing so far away, Samaira?" Amita asked.

"It's okay, aunty. I am fine here."

"But *beta...*" before Amita could say anything, Shivangi interrupted.

"It's fine, Mom. I'll talk to her," she gave a fake smile. When Shivangi's mom went to greet others, Shivangi questioned Samaira on her behaviour.

"It is not like that, Shivangi. I have to go back on 14th November, as my classes start on 17th November. And the pandemic isn't over yet. I know it's your birthday. But it feels like everyone has forgotten that the virus still exists," Samaira sighed. She was a medical student. She knew that there was going to be a rough second wave and seeing everyone unaware of the situation made her sad.

"Anyhow, you go and cut the cake. I'll be here."

Shivangi felt sad, but she understood her point of view and smiled at her. She nodded and called out for everyone.

"Okay, guys. Let's cut the cake," she shouted in excitement, and everyone cheered.

***

After everyone went home, Shivangi and her family were having dinner when her father spoke, "So, you didn't ask about your gift."

"Gift? There's a gift?" she asked in excitement.

Her father nodded, and she started jumping, "Where is it?"

Everyone else smiled and looked at each other, and then her mother told her about their plan for a family vacation. It had been long since they left their house. So, they thought they would go to Delhi and meet their family and spend some time with everyone. The family was travelling for the first time during the pandemic. Her grandma, aunts, uncles, brothers, and sisters, everyone was going to be at a single place after a long time. Shivangi was on cloud nine. She kept thanking her family, along with asking them to plan as soon as possible.

Shivangi was excited. She had started packing as soon as her father said that the ticket was confirmed. Her wardrobe was empty as her clothes were lying on the bed, dumped in the suitcase, and scattered on the floor.

"What are you even doing?" her mother asked. She was horrified seeing the mess. She started cleaning it but gave up as Shivangi kept throwing more clothes on the bed. "You don't have to pack a lot of clothes. We are going for a few days only. Now clear this mess," her mother said and left her daughter in the messy room.

***

The weather in Delhi was freezing, and everyone was either wearing a sweater or a scarf. Shivangi was having a cup of coffee. She looked around at her family and smiled. She realised how happy she was at that moment.

They were all staying at her aunt Jiya's place. She was her father's younger sister, and she had a daughter, Myra.

It has been a few days since they reached here. They had brought three cakes on the first day to celebrate all the birthdays and anniversaries they missed. And later, spent the whole evening at McDonald's. It was Myra's favourite place. And no one could say no to the youngest member of the family. The next day, they all stayed home and ordered different varieties of food for breakfast, lunch, and dinner. The next day, they went out for meals at restaurants and shopped at the mall. Shivangi realised that half of the people she noticed didn't even wear masks. They carried it with them but maybe to be safe from the police. She even noticed that no one followed social distancing. It was almost like they had all forgotten about the virus.

They all gathered in the hall of her aunt's apartment, having a cup of tea together. Today was the last day of their trip. They had thoroughly enjoyed it, and Shivangi felt rejuvenated after the much-needed outing. "This is so peaceful. We all are together. It feels like we are back in our lives. No virus, no stress, nothing," said Amita.

Everyone laughed and joked about it. Yet again, Shivangi fell into deep thought. In the background, she could hear everyone sharing stories about the past few months while she was thinking about the words her mother had said, "No virus."

Is the virus really gone? she thought.

"My brother is planning the wedding of his daughter next month, but we are telling them to postpone it. They are inviting me too, but I won't go, looking at the situation," Amita's voice brought her back to the conversation.

"I know, people think that the virus is a joke," her aunt replied.

Shivangi put down her cup and went out to the balcony, thinking about all the articles she had read. *Did some people think this virus is a joke? Does this virus exist?* She thought. Once, she had read that people from towns and villages believed that this virus was an illusion, or a lie made up by the rich people so that the poor could suffer loss and die. That didn't make any sense to her.

She looked at her family, happy and smiling through the window. She thought about how people were roaming free and enjoying lives as if the virus had disappeared. Everyone was celebrating their freedom after a few months of staying at home. She then remembered her mother talking about her cousin's marriage. Marriage! It was the wedding season during winters in India. People chose to wear masks only to match them with their clothes, to look fashionable. Talking about weddings and social distance in one sentence sounds like the biggest joke ever. Weddings are like festivals. Coming to festivals, they have added that string of hope in everyone, so much that they have forgotten to say safe. It feels like staying safe and taking precautions for one's own life has become a formality.

With this pandemic, we have realised that there are two different ends of the world. One accepts and moves on, and the other neglects to move on. It was tiresome in the beginning, but like a video game, we warmed up. We levelled up, and now everything seemed normal. Like the virus doesn't exist, or maybe we have accepted life with this virus, she thought.

Cancelled
TOKYO 2020

10

THE YEAR OF DISASTERS?

"From happiness to sorrow, human beings have to go from all the phases of life, whether they like it or not. Who would have thought there would come a year which may change everything, forever? Or is this year too overrated? Don't you think we are too much into it that we forget there will be better years than this one? Let's say this year didn't exist."

Shivangi was writing her diary when her phone beeped with a message. She never checked her messages when she was in the middle of writing, but today she felt like she should. As soon as she saw the name, her eyes lit up. It was Varun, one of her childhood friends. Varun used to live in her colony until he had to go to Australia for further studies. After a few years, his family shifted to a new house. She put her pen in the book, closed the book, took her phone, and sat on her bed.

She opened his chat. It said, "I've been in India for a while, want to meet?"

"What?" Shivangi shouted in excitement, so loudly that today she woke her mom and had to listen to her scolding for five whole minutes. Ayaansh was enjoying the show. He was laughing and adding comments in the middle. Finally, after her mom left, she skidded Ayaansh away and opened the chat. There was another message, "I know we have not talked for a while but leaving me on read is a little mean." It ended with an emoji that meant that he was teasing her.

She chuckled and replied, "Sorry, mom was scolding…" she typed but then backspaced it. She didn't want him to know that she got scolded as a 22-year-old woman. It may be common in India, but Varun had moved to Australia after his 12th class and has lived there for almost seven years. He was accustomed to the Australian lifestyle. She retyped, stating that she got busy and that she would love to meet him. Varun responded immediately, and both decided to meet at a cafe.

Shivangi was very excited to meet him after so long. She had decided the dress she would wear, with all the matching accessories. She was always a comfort-first person, but that day she wanted to look good. She had asked the opinion of her best friends, of course. And Diuja and Samaira left no chance of teasing her. And she, not even wanting to, blushed a lot. Even Ayaansh would keep teasing her, now and then, but all she said was that they were good friends and meeting after an awfully long time. Varun was four years older than her and much more mature, so she chose a plain and sophisticated outfit. That day she slept with a broad smile on her face.

The next morning was like a new experience altogether. She was supposed to meet him at 11 in the morning. It was a Sunday. But the dress that Shivangi had chosen was perfect only on the bed, not on herself. She changed so many clothes and finally gave up and decided to wear a simple black jumpsuit. Her wardrobe was filled with black, so she opted for her lucky colour. She was still a bit upset about the dress fiasco. But as soon as she reached the cafe and saw him, her nervousness was gone, and all she felt was happiness in her heart. She didn't know why she was so happy to meet him. But she went and stood in front of him and forwarded her hand for a handshake.

"Hi, I am Shivangi, and you are?" she asked as if meeting a stranger.

Varun looked up, and he was hypnotised. Shivangi looked beautiful.

She had grown so much in the last seven years. They both followed each other on social media, but the reality was always different and better. She was feeling a bit awkward. She clicked her fingers in front of him and offered her hand again.

"Shivangi," she emphasised.

Varun shook out of his daze. He looked at her hand and then her eyes. He clasped her hands in his, but rather than going for a handshake, he pulled her and took her in a hug. She was shocked, but then she realised it might be common for foreigners to greet people like that. She awkwardly patted his back and broke the hug. They both looked flustered. They found a cosy table and sat opposite each other. It was an outside cafe.

"So, how have you been?" she asked.

"I am great, as you can see. How are you?" he chuckled. His Australian accent was as clear as crystal.

"I am good too. For now, I am starving. Let's order?"

"Sure," he said as he skimmed through the menu, and she did so too. He would keep stealing glances at her. Soon the waiter came, and they both placed their respective orders.

"So, what's up with you? It has been so long. How is everything going?" he started this time.

"Well, as you might know, the pandemic has turned our life upside down. Not many tournaments, online college, and staying at home, that's life," she shrugged.

"Yes, a lot of things have changed," Varun said as he looked at her. It seemed like he meant something else, but she continued the conversation.

"Yeah. What a year it has been," she replied. Shivangi thought what she should say next when Varun asked, "Hey, do you mind? Until our orders come, I'll puff a cig and come."

"What?" Shivangi was confused.

"You know I am a bit nervous, need to smoke," he replied, embarrassed.

"Since when do you smoke?"

"Since a few years."

She raised her eyebrows, listening to his answer. When she expressed her disappointment, Varun told her that he had picked up this habit in Australia, and even though he tried to quit, he wasn't able to.

"Of course, go ahead. Who am I to stop you?" Shivangi shrugged, but her expressions said a different story.

Varun sighed. He promised that he would try harder to quit, but right now, he needed it. She shrugged again. He got up and went to a little far corner while she sat there and watched him. When he returned, their order had arrived, but the environment was a little tense. He took her hands in his, and in that single moment, she felt butterflies. She wasn't even listening while he kept on promising that he would surely quit. She unknowingly nodded, and he left her hand. That's when her trance broke. She let go of the topic and asked about his journey back.

"Well, I was not willing to come, but you know my family was worried about me. I was in Australia in January, and the pandemic started here in March. I had to rush to India. I quit my job there and came here."

"Oh, yes, your job. What did you do exactly?"

"Seriously?"

"Actually, I have been so busy, and we weren't even in touch, so I have forgotten."

Varun stared at her but replied, "Well, I am an accountant."

"Oh, I see, so you worked for a company there?"

"Yes, but now I work for our business, my family business. We have our factory here. I handle the accounts altogether."

"I didn't know that you are managing the factory. That is great." Shivangi said, trying to hide the excitement in her voice. She hoped that he would keep working at the factory and never leave.

"Basically, I just work for them."

"You should keep working here. At least you are occupied here during this pandemic before going back to Australia."

"This is the plan, for now. When I was there, everyone in my family was panicking. They wanted me to come here as soon as possible because my visa was ending, and my parents were worried about me."

Varun then told her about his journey back. Before departure, he got tested, but thankfully, it was negative. Later, when he arrived at the destination, he had to get a thermal scan at the airport. He then had to stay in a government hostel as they asked him to get isolated for fifteen days. Though, they were letting people go after two days.

"I had to stay there for two days as they had taken my passport."

Shivangi understood. She told him about her friends who had travelled during that time too. She asked him about Australia. He said that it was pretty similar in all places of the world. They all had panicked, and the only difference was that the necessities, mainly groceries and toilet paper, were sold out soon.

"One thing I realised in the pandemic is that no matter how much money you have, you are still going to die," added Varun.

He told her different incidents where people spent a tremendous amount of money but still couldn't save their loved ones.

"One of our far distanced relatives, a family of three. They all were tested positive and were hospitalised. My maternal cousin uncle got a call from the hospital to bring a cheque of around fifty lakhs for their treatment, as they were not able to pay fully. He managed to pay twenty lakhs but unfortunately, they all died."

"What? The whole family of three died?"

"Yes, sadly, they died, and the money was of no use. These hospitals are just taking advantage. I have rarely seen anyone going to the hospital and returning."

"Well, you are right. Even, I think the same."

"Anyways, I have learned this lesson now. I have lost a few family members and close friends. I now feel like enjoying every moment of life. I want to be with my family, travel, and live in the present because you never know when you have to say goodbye to this life. No property or money can help you. Life is unpredictable, Shivangi," said Varun. He seemed like he was on the verge of tearing up. She didn't know how to react. She stayed silent and just put her hands on his and said nothing. They both stayed silent for a while as Varun composed himself.

"Everything got cancelled this year. The festivals were around the corner. The enthusiasm was high. I remember enjoying on Holi, and then suddenly we were caged at our homes," she said, changing the topic.

They both sat and discussed all that the world has seen in the span of one year.

It started with the Australian bushfire that led to the burn of forty-six million acres of land and eighty percent of world heritage. Nature went berserk on the world this year. The Amphan cyclone affected the regions of Calcutta and Odisha to floods and earthquakes. The explosion in Beirut killed so many people and left lakhs of people homeless. Yemen was in the middle of a civil war. In 2020, more than 2,500 major fires burned across the Brazilian Amazon between late May and early November.

Even the Olympics and IPL were delayed. It felt like the one thing that gave humans little happiness was taken away from them.

"We would never have thought that a dead body will have to wait for cremation," Shivangi exclaimed.

Varun remained silent for a few seconds, then replied, "This year has been a lot harsher to us. The pandemic, the disasters, the protests among humans, natural calamities. Who knows what will happen next?"

He went on to say that he believed among everything that happened, they have certainly changed. Being more sensitive towards life. The gratefulness for the smallest things. To stay humble as no human is superior and there is no partisanship to natural disasters and pandemics.

Varun was still explaining his perspective when Shivangi stated that he was being too philosophical. He ignored her remark and continued.

"We are suffering together because a pandemic or a disaster never differentiates between the rich or poor," he completed.

"I understand, Varun, but let us look at it this way. You know Varun, I feel like 2020 has been the year of disasters, blessings in disguise, and it gave us a feeling of lose, fear and gratitude, we loved our loved ones, felt their pain, we craved for our freedom and a lot more! The year taught us to finally accept the changes which were required to be accepted long before! The year has been different and has tested our fortitude!" Shivangi said in one go.

"Wow! That's deep," Varun was astonished by her perspective. His intense gaze made her blush, and when he noticed that, he chuckled. "A little while ago, you were calling me philosophical. Now, who's being philosophical?"

"Well, it is your effect, I assume," Shivangi smirked, and they both laughed.

The way people look at the world has changed. Not taking even the smallest things for granted. Who knew that this would bring a drastic change in the world?

"A pandemic can definitely change a person. I mean, look at me, my career shifted from being an accountant in Australia to working for my family business here."

"Even I am exploring my passion for writing," she beamed, and he gave her a breath-taking smile.

They sat silent for a while, staring at each other when Shivangi's phone rang. It was her mother calling to ask her when she was returning. Shivangi sighed. *If your mom doesn't call when you go out, then she is not an Indian mom,* she thought to herself.

They both stood up and hugged again. As they paid the bill, Shivangi asked, "So when are we meeting again?" Varun shrugged and chuckled. "Whenever you say, but I'll be leaving for Australia in two months or something," he said so casually that her heart broke. She assumed that he would stay back, and they would keep meeting, but all her dreams were shattered. She simply nodded, and they both went their separate ways.

Shivangi sat with her diary again. It was after dinner.

"What the year 2020 had brought for us, can we call it nature's gift or a curse?" she wrote.

"Whom to blame for all the destructions and what else to expect from our near future?

There's a need for us to remind ourselves that these natural calamities and destruction keep occurring almost every year. Maybe we are noticing it well enough, considering we all are already going through a pandemic.

The year of disaster is '1672' considered by the historians, and history might again repeat itself. Who knows?

One valuable lesson we learned is that nothing is more important than your health and family. We have understood the value of our families, the importance of our environment, and the privilege we have," she closed her book and kept it aside as she replayed her conversation with Varun. She thought about him going back and understood that even if the year of disasters had passed for others, it was still the year of disaster for her.

11

A LESSON FOR THE LIFETIME

It was a chilly winter night. Everyone had gathered for the new year's party at Shivangi's house. Samaira's parents joined, but Samaira couldn't as she was at her college hostel. Shivangi's neighbours, Sonali, Akshara, and their younger brother Kiaan joined, with their parents. It was their idea to have a new year's party. Even Shivangi's cousin sister, Ruchika, who lived in the same city as hers, joined them with her husband Saurav and their two kids. Everyone had come together after so long.

"We were so frustrated at home, all isolated and nowhere to go. Finally, we all stepped out of the house. The plan of staying the night is great. We needed some change," said Ruchika, as they sat cosily in the veranda.

"I understand, *beta*. That is why I called you. I am happy you came," said Amita.

Shivangi and Ruchika were maternal cousins. Both of their mothers were sisters.

"Yes, we were relieved after our father recovered, but it was a challenging time for all of us."

"We can understand. When exactly did everything happen?"

It was Saurav who replied, "It happened in November. We had Diwali celebrations at our house, a lot of people had gathered during that time. After a few days, dad was not feeling well. He was feeling weak and had a fever. We all were panicked. We were more worried because, at the age of seventy-six, you never know what might happen, and this was the novel coronavirus. I called our family doctor, who is also a friend of mine, he suggested that he should take the Covid test."

The party was filled with silence as he continued, "First, we had the Rapid Antigen test. We all had to stay away from him. He was tested positive in the RTPCR test on the same day. It came as a shock to all of us. I was scared for my father's health. It was nothing less than a nightmare for me," he paused for a second as if replaying those times.

"The next day, the government nurse came to check his oxygen level. It was around 86-87%. They suggested we take a CT scan. After the scan, unfortunately, we got to know that his lungs had been 70-80% damaged, and his oxygen level was already less than 90%. That shook us to the core. We admitted him to a private hospital immediately."

"What happened then?" Shivangi asked, both in curiosity and worry.

"We had to admit him in ICU. The admission fee was thirty- two thousand rupees, but we had no other options. We didn't want to delay the treatment any further," he said, and Shivangi's eyes grew as wide as saucers while the adults just nodded along. When Saurav told them further about the cost of the remdesivir injection, which was around forty thousand for six injections, her eyes grew wider. It cost them a total of seventy- two thousand for the treatment. The medical staff said it would take around two to fifteen days to recover, but as he felt better after two to three days, they shifted him to a government hospital where they had to pay another twenty-one thousand for the admission. Finally, almost after a week, when Saurav's father felt much better, they brought him home.

"How was the situation at home?" asked Amita. The supposed fun party was now taking a serious turn. "We were tensed, panicked, and terrorised. After we brought him home, he had to get quarantined. He stayed in a room upstairs while we all stayed down. He was scared too. He didn't want to eat anything. But somehow, we managed to give him some healthy fruit and vegetable juice. I still remember that one night," he said as he went into a flashback of that night.

*****

November 2020

Saurav's dad was shifted to the government hospital. The situation was tense. But they were relaxed that he was recovering.

It was around 2 AM when Saurav got a call. He didn't recognise the number. But he picked it up immediately. He wouldn't miss any calls at night, considering anything could be of emergency during this time.

"Hello, is this Saurav?" asked the person on the other side.

"Yes. It is. Who is this?" Saurav questioned back.

"I am the nurse from the hospital. Your father asked me to ring you up. He is not looking well," was the answer. The nurse, during his duties, would often give his phone to the patients so that they could connect with their families.

Saurav went into a frenzy. He sat upright on the bed, which disturbed Ruchika's sleep, as well. And she knew from Saurav's expression that the call was from the hospital.

"What happened? Is he alright? Can you pass him the phone?" he said as he gave a worried look to Ruchika. He heard a little shuffling, and the next moment his father spoke on the call.

"Saurav, *beta*, I am feeling very lonely, and I am very scared," he said, his voice breaking with every word.

That evening, he got to know that the patient on the bed beside him, who was having his Covid treatment, had died.

"Sir, relax. You are panicking. See, you are sweating a lot," Saurav could hear the nurse saying in the background. His father was stuttering. He couldn't even utter the words clearly. But one thing was clear, that he wanted to come back.

"I can't stay here for one more day. Come and take me home," he said with tears in his eyes.

"Stay strong, Dad. You are staying there only so you can recover well." Saurav gave hope to his father while he was himself so scared that he rushed down to his car, Ruchika had poured tea in a thermos, and Saurav left for the hospital. He couldn't go in, but he stood outside the hospital. All the while being on call and assuring his father that everything would be fine, that he was just outside the hospital.

But his father wouldn't stop stressing. The fear of death had gripped him. Seeing someone die beside him was a terrible incident.

"Dad, it's a hospital. Someone dying is normal. You don't think about it. Take god's name and sleep. I promise I will get you discharged tomorrow morning," Saurav comforted his father.

He requested the nurse and asked him if he could come down there, outside the hospital, to which he agreed. Saurav had to wait for a few minutes, which to him felt like hours. His mind was filled with constant thoughts of his father. His father's words and worries rang in his ears. But he had to stay strong. He had to think positively. He shook off his thoughts as he saw the nurse approach.

"Here," Saurav handed him the thermos. "Give it to my father and tell him that I will be here. He doesn't have to worry," he said with pleading eyes.

"Okay, sir. You don't have to worry. You sit there on the bench and stay strong. He is a fighter; he will be okay," the nurse consoled. He had been very helpful. Whenever he was on duty, he would help in sending food to his father.

Saurav spent the whole night on the bench outside the hospital.

He called Ruchika and informed her about the situation. Both stayed awake the whole night worrying about their father's health. The next morning, as promised, Saurav asked the doctor for his father's discharge, and seeing his recovery speed, he was discharged on the note that he had to be self-quarantined at their home. His father was overjoyed seeing Saurav and the news that he was going home or maybe because he wouldn't die in the hospital bed.

***

Present

"He coped up with all these pretty well. I must say, he has a very strong mind and heart," said Amita.

"Yes, he does. But that night still haunts him. When he was home-quarantined, he kept the lights on while sleeping. He mostly stayed in the balcony and drank tea. We were careful about everything. We would keep his food on the stairs, and he would take it from there. Even after he was back home, I often stood outside our house, so he could see me from the balcony. Sometimes post-midnight and sometimes till two in the morning. We would often talk the whole night on days he couldn't sleep."

"Those were the toughest times of our lives," interrupted Ruchika.

"My father recovered in ten to fifteen days, but the expenses we bear can be someone's life earnings. He didn't want to stay in the hospital. He begged me to bring him home after two days, but I couldn't, his treatment was important, but after that night, I had to bring him home."

The environment had become gloomy. Everyone sat there sadly when Saurav spoke again.

"But I am telling you, everything is about fear. You can conquer this virus only when you become fearless. Otherwise, it will take you with it. Everything is in our minds. When my father was in the hospital and was crying about people dying around him, I told him a few words. I said, 'If you want to live, don't think about the surroundings, close your eyes, and sleep.'"

"Wow, Saurav, you motivated and encouraged your father during nights like those. That is why he was able to recover soon. Kudos to you. You are a great son," Amita appreciated him.

"My family is the most precious thing for me. We were the happiest after he recovered. Post recovery, my father took a walk outside the house. He used to sit in the balcony and read or use his mobile phone. This experience changed him forever. I remember how worried we were for our kids when he was quarantined in a separate room. I used to clean the house, Ruchika had to work a lot, and she handled everything well. It was not less than a challenge for us as my mother has diabetes, so we had to be cautious."

"It all happened two days after Diwali. We forgot about the celebrations and went into a different zone. Isolating ourselves in the four walls had a negative impact on our mental health," Ruchika added.

"He was weak for around a month, so basically, from November to early December, we were all quarantined. We didn't know when it would end."

"It's the first day of the new year," said Sanjay as he looked at the watch; the clock struck 12. "Hopefully, everything will be normal this year," he prayed as he took a sip of his beer from the bottle.

"Finally, 2020 is over!" Ayaansh screamed in excitement, and the other kids joined in while the elders just chuckled.

"Now the old times are gone, new things will arrive this year. I am so happy and proud of you both, Ruchika and Saurav. Let's enjoy the party now. We never know what will happen tomorrow, so let's enjoy this moment," said Amita in enthusiasm.

They all laughed as they finally passed one of the toughest rocks in their lives.

After a very long time, they brought sweets from outside and even cut a cake. Everyone danced happily till two in the morning. It was one of the most fun nights for Shivangi. She thought everything was back to normal.

***

After starting with a delightful new year, everyone fell into a routine.

In a few weeks, the rumours about the vaccine finally came to rest as on 16th January, vaccines were made available for the Healthcare and frontline workers, including police, paramilitary forces, sanitation workers, and disaster management volunteers. But the fear of the second wave was growing every day. Shivangi had stopped her tennis sessions for a few days, but Ayaansh was being stubborn as usual.

It was a usual morning when Shivangi and her dad sat in the veranda, she had a cup of coffee, and he was having tea. Usually, she would read articles online, and he would scan the newspaper, but today the environment was a bit tense. Her father, rather than reading the newspaper, was rubbing his forehead. He seemed tense. When Shivangi asked what had happened, he said that his cousin who lived in Rajasthan was contaminated again.

"Again?" Shivangi asked, confused. She didn't know that Jigar was contaminated before. Her father said it was kept hidden, and only a few people knew. Even though they were cousins, Sanjay and Jigar were really close. Her father told her how Jigar was contaminated in June last year after the lockdown lifted. Sanjay said that it was all because of his carelessness. As soon as everything opened, he started going out more and never sanitised anything he brought from outside and would rarely wear a mask. He was upset with Jigar, but being the elder brother, he kept checking on him throughout the quarantine. He was able to manage then, but again in January, he went on a trip, where he was stubborn and careless, so he got contaminated again. His carelessness had always brought him troubles, and this time it was the coronavirus.

As Sanjay kept in touch with him, Jigar told them not to worry.

He assured them that he was taking care of himself. After a few days, Jigar was doing better now. He had called to talk with his brother when he recovered, and Shivangi said she wanted to talk too.

"How are you feeling now?" Shivangi asked as Sanjay handed her the phone.

"I am fine now. I am still on break and quarantined at home. How are you all?" Jigar answered. She could tell that he was weak from his voice, but there was a hint of happiness too.

"We are good and are taking good care of ourselves. We are not even stepping out of the house. I am not going to my tennis sessions either, but Ayaansh wants to go to the tennis sessions. I am trying to convince him, but you know he is stubborn. Can you please talk to him?"

"Sure."

Ayaansh stared at her and muttered, "Always complaining," before he took the phone.

"How are you, Ayaansh?" asked Jigar.

"I am fine. How are you? I am happy that you have finally recovered."

"Yes, I am much better now. I heard you plan to go to the sessions, but it is still not the right time, dear. Staying safe is the most important thing, *beta*."

Ayaansh was very annoyed with her. She always complained about him to everyone she met. He glared at her. He was not going to let her go this time, but for now, he said in a sweet voice, "Yes, uncle, I understood. I won't step out of the house unnecessarily, but I want to go to the sessions," he countered.

"I understand, *beta*, but right now, the situation is not good at all. I am telling you from my own experience."

"What exactly happened?" Ayaansh asked. He seemed a bit too excited.

"Don't take it as a joke, *beta*. This is not the right time to take things casually," Jigar said seriously.

"Yes, I understood, *Chachu*. I am not being casual. I will be staying at home until things get better," Ayaansh said, a little upset.

Shivangi knew Ayaansh didn't want to upset Jigar but just wanted to know what had happened. She took the phone from his hand and put it on speaker, and asked sympathetically, "Was the experience that bad?"

"The experience has been tremendously painful. I remember the first day when I got a fever. I had body pain, especially in the hips, and wouldn't stop coughing for a second. I had panic attacks during that time. On the second day, the pain increased. I was feeling so cold. I kept the doors and windows locked and was using three blankets, but I kept shivering the whole time."

Shivangi and Ayaansh said nothing. They kept listening and nodding from time to time. Jigar told his story in such detail that both the kids were able to understand it through his words. At one point, it felt as if Jigar would break down and cry. He was already alone, and the quarantine had made him feel lonelier and more isolated.

"This is nothing, kids. After I tested positive for the Rapid Antigen Test, my doctor suggested having a CT scan too, and I got to know about my infection in the lungs. I was so scared for my life. My fever kept increasing, and I was so weak that I couldn't even stand on my own feet or even brush. I was on heavy medications too."

Shivangi and Ayaansh looked at each other in despair, so much trouble because of a little carelessness, and then stared back at the phone screen as Jigar continued.

"That was about last year, but this year it is so different and weird. It felt like something was roaming inside my body. I could feel it from my head to my throat. It would go up and down in my body. It felt like a ghost had entered my body."

The siblings again looked at each other, and Shivangi was trying not to laugh. She felt like it was a funny comparison, but on the other hand, Ayaansh looked terrified. He mouthed to her, "I won't go for the tennis sessions," and she almost burst out laughing. She knew Ayaansh was afraid of ghosts, but she didn't know that he would take this comparison so seriously. Ayaansh glared at her again.

"Having a fever is normal, but it was a mysterious thing which happened to me. It makes things pathetic. Maybe this mysterious thing is what makes things worse. I can't describe the feeling. It felt like someone was pinching needles into my body. It hurts too much, oh my god, just thinking about it gives me goosebumps," Jigar exclaimed. "I told your dad after one week. My medication had already started by then."

"Why didn't you tell him earlier?" Shivangi asked.

"Because I didn't want to trouble him much at that time, otherwise he would have gotten too worried, and then your *Dadi* might have worried too. So, I told him after I got a little better. I didn't tell your aunt until I was better. She is in her hometown, and nor did my parents or sister knew about it. They would have panicked a lot, considering I am the sole bread earner. They might have gone into great despair. So, I decided to share it later with *bhaiya* only. He is my support and a confidant. Also, I am living alone, so they would have been tensed."

"I agree. After all, they are family. It must have been very hard for you to cope, all alone like this. Kudos to you for being so mentally strong," Ayaansh said happily.

Jigar continued telling them about how badly his own thoughts terrified him.

"At times, I even doubted whether I would recover. I even had nightmares about *Yam Raj* (God of death) coming to my dreams. It can mentally destroy any healthy person. I got thinner and couldn't eat anything. It was like I had become a rat, eating tiny bites of food."

Even though Shivangi felt upset for him, she couldn't deny that his comparisons were very weird. First ghost and now a rat.

"Who cooked when you were quarantined?" Ayaansh asked.

"Last year, your aunt was here. But this year, I was too weak. I could barely stand, so it was almost impossible for me to cook. Thankfully, I had a couple on the floor above. She would send me food through a rope on my balcony from hers as I lived below her. They helped me a lot, especially that lady. I am thankful to her. I was able to recover without any need of hospitalization, just because of her," Jigar paused, and before anyone could say anything, he said. "One thing I learned when I was lying in pain is that prevention is always better than cure. If I had taken more safety precautions, I might not have gone through this experience."

After such a long conversation. Shivangi realised how painful some life lessons can be and that Jigar had a lesson for the lifetime.

12

LOVE IN ISOLATION

Valentine's Day was around the corner, and Shivangi's thought would start with different things but ended up on Varun. Maybe he has already gone to Australia. She did not want to think of him.

I want a distraction, she thought. That is when her brain presented her with the most obvious choice, dating apps. As soon as she thought of it, something popped into her head. She shook her head. She wasn't going to download a dating app for a day.

Dating apps have changed the face of dating. Amidst this pandemic and lockdown, virtual dates are more prominent. Of course, people prefer meeting in person for their first dates. Either way, dating apps have introduced a new way to connect people with similar interests.

Today Shivangi was not even able to concentrate on writing her diary. She kept finding words to put down.

"Don't we wonder, what could have happened if the pandemic wouldn't have hit us? Maybe the loneliness wouldn't have struck us, and who knows if we had been love-struck with someone." she wrote, but when she reread her thoughts, she felt dejected. "I don't even want to write about it," she huffed and closed her diary and plopped on her bed.

She thought about her friends. Diuja had a boyfriend, and Samaira and Swastik were unofficially already together. Even though Samaira had said they were not in a relationship, Shivangi knew they would get together sooner or later. They both cared for each other. Oh, yes. She knew what she needed now. She grabbed her phone from the nightstand and video called Diuja and Samaira. Neither of them picked, but soon she got Samaira's message saying she was busy and will call in the evening, and Diuja sent a "Same here" message. Shivangi sent a rather upset okay and slumped back on the bed. She needed to talk to someone. She was getting frustrated minute by minute. She then got up and chose to disturb Ayaansh. As soon as she entered his room, he saw her and understood she was there to irritate him, and she looked upset too. Before she could even enter his room, he said, "Go and watch F.R.I.E.N.D.S. I am doing something important. Don't disturb me."

Shivangi rolled her eyes and stuck her tongue out at him, but he was right. Shivangi loved watching the series, and she had binge-watched it during the lockdown as it always calms her down and makes her laugh.

She resumed from where she was watching, and coincidently it was the episode where Phoebe talks about lobsters. She continued to watch, and as she was going to jump to the next episode, her phone rang. She thought it was Samaira or Diuja, but it was Ricky. After the social media obsession, Shivangi mostly ignored her, but soon both started talking again. Ricky's obsession had died a little as she started her bakery, or more accurately, online bakery. She had a page on Instagram, and it was doing quite well. Shivangi had seen her posts, and she loved the cake designs. She had even told Ricky about it. Even though Shivangi had not yet eaten her cakes, her page was blossoming, so she understood that Ricky was good at it.

Shivangi gratefully picked the call. She could talk to anyone right now. After the greetings, she asked about the bakery, to which Ricky told her about her messed-up schedule. Even though it was going very well, she was handling it all alone. Her parents stayed out of Mumbai most of the time, and her brother was busy with studies. She didn't have enough budget as of now to keep the staff.

"More than that, I am a clean freak and perfectionist. Honestly, I don't want anyone to mess up my things. My mom had offered to help, but I refused because I didn't want to involve people. I kind of like doing on my own," Ricky added. That reminded Shivangi of "Monica" from "F.R.I.E.N.D.S."

When Shivangi told Ricky about her comparison, they both laughed, but Ricky agreed. She was a lot like Monica. Even though handling the bakery alone exhausted her, she knew, one day, she would be able to hire a staff.

Ricky's parents travelled most of the time, so she and her brother would stay by themselves. Both were independent people. She would also cook meals herself. When Shivangi heard about all this, she felt a little awestruck and shame for herself. She didn't even enter the kitchen unless it was an emergency. When she started to compare herself with Ricky, Ricky intervened, "It is not right to compare, Shivangi. I mean, my situation has been like this since I was a kid. You have got your own skills."

Ricky's words made her feel happy as she understood that she was right. They talked about anything and everything, but one sentence caught her interest.

"Yes, I was so done with social media and so bored, I started using a dating app."

"A dating app?" Shivangi was surprised. What was happening today? All the while, she was reminded of dating only.

"Yeah. Well, I used the app for a few months. I didn't find anyone interesting enough. You know how things go here in Mumbai. People prefer flings rather than love. But I was bored, so I kept swiping."

Shivangi agreed. The current generation is always looking for dates and not for people they can spend their life with.

"Where has the loyalty gone?" Shivangi asked dispiritedly.

"Well, there are some people who can be serious, and by it, I mean damn serious."

Shivangi narrowed her eyes. "You found someone?" she asked, excited, and Ricky nodded as a light blush crept to her face.

Ricky told her about the guy she met on the app she was using. He was a student pursuing his master's in Mumbai. She went on to give a detailed description of him.

"His name is Prithvi. He is around 5'7, dusky-skinned, has smooth and curly hair. Also, his black eyes, I could literally swim in them," Ricky said as her face turned redder. Shivangi just cooed and awed.

Prithvi was a musician. He played Ukulele, a four-stringed guitar. Shivangi readily asked for his picture. She wanted to see what her friend's date looked like. Ricky agreed but made her promise that she wouldn't send it to anyone else, to which Shivangi nodded.

Ricky had found many guys on the app, but no one seemed genuine until she matched with him. Both had the same reason to join the app because they were bored. The one thing that attracted her was that he wasn't looking for a casual fling. She did think about the chance that he might be bluffing, but their conversations were always friendly. She vibed well with him. A few weeks later, they shared their Instagram IDs. She wasn't comfortable sharing her number yet. The best part was, Prithvi had neither asked for the Instagram ID nor her number, but it was Ricky who trusted him.

They continued their daily conversations on Instagram throughout the lockdown. A week before the lockdown was about to end, they were texting when Ricky accidentally clicked the video call. As soon as she realised it, she cut the call and clarified that it was a clear mistake. Prithvi told her that if she was comfortable, then they could have a video call, and she agreed. Maybe it was the pull. She wanted to see him face to face, even if it was on the phone. She quickly untied her hair and called him. He picked up in less than a second. He was wearing a grey T-shirt, and his curly hairs were unruly. He looked like the god of cuteness. She couldn't help but blush, and in return, he blushed too, which made him more adorable.

"Wow, so dreamy," Shivangi interrupted Ricky and brought her back from her dreamland. She had forgotten that she was narrating her story. She felt as if she was living it all over again. She told Shivangi not to interrupt again with a red face, and Shivangi nodded childlike.

Prithvi and Ricky had a great conversation that day. They even decided that they would meet after the lockdown opened. She found that he lived only a few kilometres away. When everything opened, both decided to meet at a cafe. Ricky was absolutely on cloud nine. They spent the next two hours chatting, and when it was time to leave, Prithvi sweetly gave his phone to her and asked, "Can I have your number please?" she was wonderstruck. She was ecstatic. She added her number to his phone and gave herself a call as well.

"It has almost been around nine months since we are talking. After that day at the cafe, we meet almost every other weekend. I am busy with my bakery, and he, with his studies. We don't get too much time for each other, but I am glad that we both are in the same city."

"The effort you both put in is more important. You guys are meeting regularly, which is a great effort from both of you. Sometimes long-distance messes things."

"True that. That is why I am happy that he is from the same city."

Prithvi had a few similar interests too. He loves baking and is a dog lover like Ricky. He had met her pets Poko and Donut, and they loved him too. The mere thought of him made her happy.

"Thank God, I was in the lockdown and got a chance to meet Prithvi," she said happily.

Shivangi was surprised to know that people can meet on dating apps and have a love story. Ricky told Shivangi about her senior, who too found love during the lockdown and was getting married soon. They talked about the wedding season that happened during the lockdown. Every other day someone was getting married.

"We can say love in isolation is much sweeter than anything else," Ricky smiled, thinking of Prithvi.

Shivangi nodded, but now she was more intrigued to use a dating app, "Ricky, how do these dating apps work?"

"You have to make your profile and swipe right for the people you like. If it's a match, you get to talk to the person. You need to enable your location for that. Mostly the app can cover almost every area in the city."

"Wow. That sounds easy and fun."

"Do you want to use it too, Shivangi?" Ricky wiggled her eyebrows, and Shivangi laughed it off. She said she wasn't thinking of it, but Ricky saw through her lie.

"See, I am not a technically savvy person, but I love this dating app thing. I mean, you can even find your soulmate," Ricky tried to convince her.

"Although, Ricky, maybe you are expecting a lot. I mean, we are young, we can fall in love, but we can't be sure of the future," Shivangi said.

"I know, but this is pretty serious. I mean, we can't think about the consequences every time we date. Prithvi is a nice guy. I am happy to have found him on a dating app."

"I see, but make sure of any red flags."

"Shivangi, you need to talk to him once. I know the times are tough, but I trust this guy. I have given enough time to know him now," Ricky said and then sighed. "Sure. It's your choice. But even in isolation, I found my companion. I found my lobster," she added and blushed.

"Ricky, you can't stop blushing," Shivangi chuckled. "And I love Phoebe. I binged watched a lot of shows including 'Friends.'"

Ricky readily nodded. She told Shivangi about how she and Prithvi would watch series together sometimes on video calls or keep track of what episode they both were on.

"If any one of us goes ahead by an episode, we get upset. Sometimes, distance makes it more fun, but as long as we are in the same city. It's not a problem."

Shivangi nodded, and then Ricky said that she had to plan something for Prithvi as Valentine's Day was approaching, so she needed to go. They both said bye, and now Shivangi was more confused than before about dating apps. *Should I download it? No, first, let me talk to Samu and Diu,* she thought.

***

She spent the rest of her day watching series. After dinner, she was in her room when she got a call from both Samaira and Diuja. They greeted each other, and Shivangi told them about her day and the urge to download a dating app.

"See, Shivangi, Shrant and I knew each other from school times, and we fell in love gradually," said Diuja.

"Yes, even Swastik and I know each other from college. But yes, we did start our relationship from this pandemic and lockdown," added Samaira.

Shivangi hummed as she thought about both of their relationships. Diuja and Shrant were classmates from when they were in the first standard. Soon, they became best friends and now a couple. They have grown together as people. Shrant lived in Bangalore, and Diuja was in Lucknow, but they managed their relationship pretty well.

"First of all, I am not so fond of these dating apps as you know I am an old school romantic. Though I know a few people who met on these apps and are serious about each other," Diuja kept her opinion.

Shivangi remembered what happened with Diuja and Shrant last year during the lockdown. They both had started to have more arguments due to long-distance, and they both decided to break up.

But within a month, they both suffered more than when they were together. When they came back together, their bond grew stronger. They realised how much they missed each other, and the value for their love increased.

"The distance brought us closer," Diuja had said then.

Shrant was tested positive for Covid after a few days of them getting back together. Diuja was more worried than him. That time brought them so much closer.

"You are absolutely right. Though with love comes trust. You have known Shrant for more than ten years. You can trust him, but how can you trust a person you meet on the internet."

"I understand. Trust comes with time. But sometimes you can meet a person and instantly know that they are the right person for you," Diuja said, and Shivangi agreed. Both were engrossed in talking that they didn't notice the silence of Samaira. When they looked over, they saw that she was smiling and blushing, but she wasn't paying attention to the call. When Shivangi looked closer, she realised that Samaira was texting someone. Shivangi looked at Diuja, and they both smirked. Shivangi held up three fingers and counted down to one, and then both shouted together, "SAMAIRA!"

Samaira almost dropped her phone, and both of them laughed.

"You, stupid people. Why are you shouting?" she exclaimed.

"Because you are busy with your Mr. Right when we have an important conversation here," said Shivangi.

Samaira was embarrassed. She quickly left him a text and then gave her full concentration to her two idiot friends. Shivangi and Diuja filled her on the topic of conversation. Samaira didn't have much to add, but she agreed with Diuja about "the right person" point.

"See, Shivangi, it's ultimately your choice. But whatever it may be, like an arranged marriage, online dating, childhood love, you have to take a leap of faith," Samaira said, and Diuja nodded. Shivangi nodded too. She knew Samaira was right about it.

It was already too late, and both Diuja and Samaira wanted to go and talk to their "lovers." So, they all said their goodnight.

Shivangi thought about Samaira and Swastik as she remembered when she got the chance to talk to him a few weeks ago.

***

January 2021

After reminding Samaira every day, Shivangi finally got the chance to talk to Swastik.

Samaira was back from her hostel for a few days. Shivangi went to Samaira's house, feeling overwhelmed, as they had scheduled a conversation with Swastik. It was Sunday. He was free and relaxed.

"Hey. Someone wants to talk to you," Samaira said on the call and handed the phone to Shivangi.

"Hey," Shivangi exclaimed in excitement.

"Hello," Swastik replied softly.

"Wow, I am talking to you for the very first time. How are you?"

"Yeah," he chuckled, listening to her excitement, "I am good. How are you, Shivangi?"

"I am doing pretty good. Well, your girlfriend doesn't stop talking about you, and she blushes a lot."

"Well, she is an angel, you know, and they look pretty when they blush."

"Aww, you are so sweet, Swastik. No wonder why she keeps bragging about you."

"I don't brag," Samaira interrupted.

"Yes, you do, sometimes," both Swastik and Shivangi said in unison.

"Well, you keep asking about him, so I will have to," Samaira defended as her face kept turning redder by the minute.

As the phone was on speaker, Swastik intervened, "Girls, it's okay, don't argue, and there is no need to brag about me. I am who I am. I am not a superhero."

"Well, you are one. You are a real-life superhero," Shivangi exclaimed again.

"Ha-ha, not really," he laughed.

"No, you are, I mean it. Look how hard you work for us every single day. It is the most incredible thing one can do for society."

"Well again, I would say, it is my duty. I am not obliged to do anything. This is my life. I chose it and will continue to do so."

Shivangi was awestruck with his confession. She adored him even more now. They talked for a little more while, then Swastik had to go, but before disconnecting, she added, "Also, Samaira misses you a lot."

"I know how much my little angel cares about me. She is love."

Samaira blushed again. Shivangi passed the phone back to her.

"He is at least relaxed today," she said, hanging up the phone.

"He is a hard worker and a sweet guy. I really like him."

"He doesn't like talking on calls, but he did talk to you."

"He is the right guy for you."

"I know," Samaira chuckled.

***

Present

Shivangi thought about Samaira's point of view about taking a leap of faith. She realised how many people had taken that leap of faith during a time when hope was dying every day and found their love in isolation.

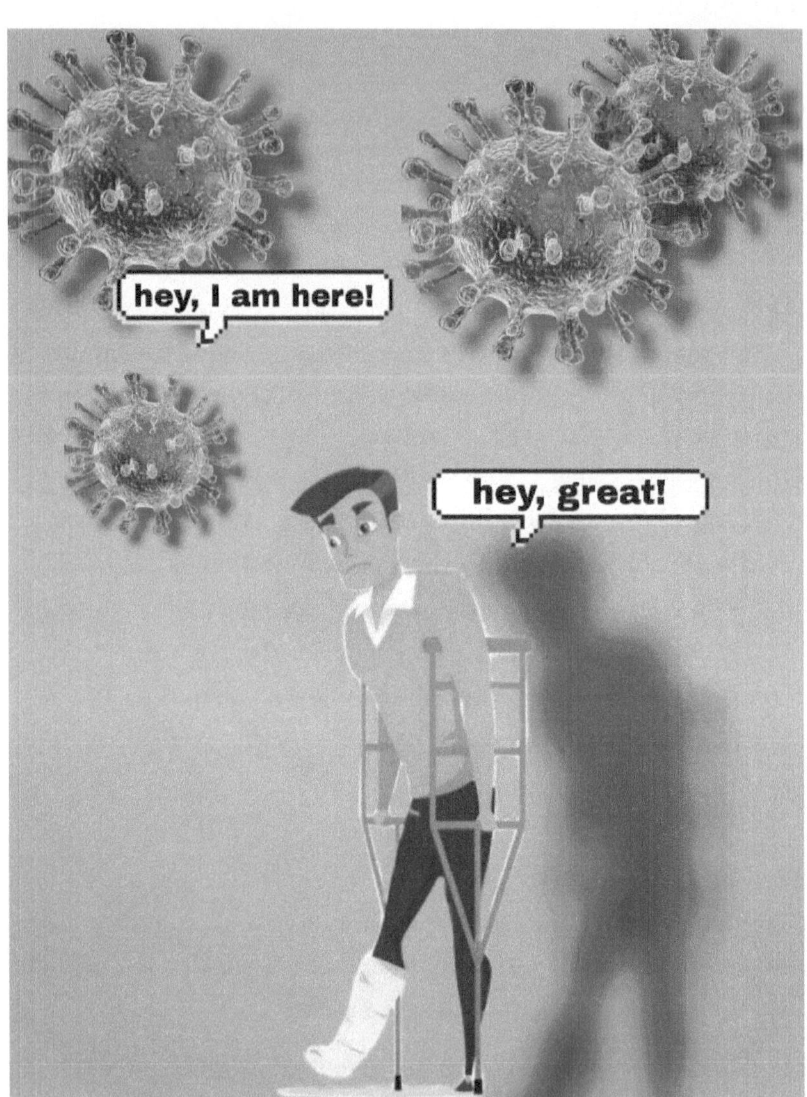

hey, I am here!
hey, great!

13

WORSE THAN COVID?

It has been a year since the first wave of the pandemic started. Throughout the year, everyone hoped that things would get better. But now, here they were. Fearing that the happening of the last year might repeat itself. Shivangi had reconnected with so many of her old friends and relatives. She felt like it was why she could get through the year. She was thinking about all this when she got a notification. It was an old friend, Sumit. He was an athlete, but their friendship had started because of books. Both loved reading books and would discuss every new book they read. But as lockdown started, Shivangi's reading habit fell a little. She got busy taking care of herself and writing. They both texted for a while. She got to know that his habit of reading books had skyrocketed, and he had a book collection too. She was very intrigued, and she asked him if he could show her his collection, and he eagerly said yes. His exact words were, "Of course, other than buying and reading books, showing my book collection to others makes me happier."

Shivangi was eager too. They decided they would video call each other. As soon as Shivangi picked up the call, she didn't say hello or hi but asked about his bookshelf. Her excitement was on another level. He had a whole shelf of books from different, versatile authors.

"This is my collection. I am not sure if you have heard about these authors before," he spoke.

"Of course not. You are a bigger bibliophile here. Though, you still don't have my favourite book with you," she laughed.

"Which one?" he asked, raising his eyebrows.

"You know it, 'The Alchemist.'" she exclaimed.

"Oh yes, I don't have that, but I have other books of the same author, let me show you," he said. She felt like his voice was cracking. It sounded low and hoarse.

"Hey, what happened to your voice? You sound a bit off. Is everything alright?" she asked, and when she looked closer at his face, she could see he looked a bit weak, too.

"Why do you look weak?" she asked.

"It is probably nothing. I recovered from Covid a few days ago. Maybe I still have a little weakness," he answered casually, and she was stunned.

"And when were you planning to tell me this? When did all this happen?" she said, both upset and sympathetically.

"Calm down, please. I am sorry, but I didn't tell any of my friends. I felt a little embarrassed. Also, I didn't want any sympathy from anyone. I will tell you the whole story. Just don't get annoyed, okay?" he said, and she sighed. He looked too weak to be mad on.

"Fine, I won't be mad, but why do you feel embarrassed? What is wrong with that?" she asked, confused.

"It's just, I got contaminated, and the people around might mock me."

"Dude, why will anyone mock you? We are your friends. I mean, you are not a criminal, and you didn't get infected deliberately." she said the last part to herself.

"I know Shivangi, but still, after getting infected, there were people who looked down at me, though you are right, not all people behaved that way. Some were helpful too. Thank you for consoling me."

"Shut up, Sumit. I am your friend. So now tell me what happened?"

she asked in excitement. Her inner writer was always looking for stories in the world.

"One day, mom and I were having breakfast. As you know, dad lives in a different city, we both live alone in our apartment. She wasn't feeling well. She said that she needed to get tested as soon as possible. She was all worried and scared that she might have the virus. I tried to convince her that it might be a little fever or something, but she didn't budge. For her satisfaction, we both got tested. First, we had the Rapid Antigen Test. In ten minutes, the result came, and it was positive. We both were shocked as we both were tested positive. Mom panicked and got more tensed."

Sumit went on to talk about his experience. He said his mom was panicking, and they decided to get tested again, only to confirm. For that, they chose to go to the hospital. They went a little later in the evening, and fortunately, it wasn't crowded, but there were people all around who had Covid, and he and his mom were terrified. He had to stay tough for his mother as she was on the verge of being unconscious. Stress had taken a toll on her. He told Shivangi about a guy who had lost his father, and he and his brother were positive. He kept coughing, and Sumit was worried for his mother.

"There was a mental picture of that guy and his family in my mind when I was returning home. It wasn't easy at all. Plus, mom was worried about being tested positive. She had too many tantrums. Why can't she stay strong during these times?"

"It is okay, Sumit. Anyone can panic during this kind of situation. After all, she is your mother. She was worried about your health too. Don't call it tantrums. When someone gets tested positive for such infectious disease, they can lose their senses. That was very insensitive of you to call your mother like that." Shivangi felt upset over his comment.

"Yes, you are right. I understand. It's just that I was too irritated at that time. My mom was being too weak considering the situation.

I wished she could have stayed stronger and stable."

Shivangi nodded, but she was still upset with him. Both Sumit and his mom were quarantined for fifteen days. He recovered fast, but his mom took longer.

"I guess I have better immunity. As you know, I am an athlete," he said.

He told about his quarantine days. When he would read books and clean the house or do home chores. His mom would make breakfast. For lunch and dinner, the watchman's wife would send homemade food.

"His wife helped us during these tough times, especially sending us food. Though, I had lost my taste and smell. I am thankful to her," he added.

"I understand. It must have been tough for you," she said sympathetically.

"To be honest, I was chilled out. I wasn't bothered or worried because I have seen even worse things in my life. That was probably nothing compared to that," he said confidently.

"Something worse than Covid?" she asked, surprised.

"Not a lot of people know about it, except my girlfriend and a few friends."

"Well, of course, Pisha would know. How is she?"

"She is totally fine. She kept checking on me during these tough times, and you know this long-distance suck, but she didn't leave me alone even for a moment."

"It's great to hear. Touchwood, I would say. I am so happy for both of you. She really loves you."

"Yes, and so do I."

"Alright, Mr. Romeo, can you please continue the story now," Shivangi said and then added a soft. "And stop blushing," to which his face turned red, and she laughed.

"I am not blushing. Anyway, the thing is, I had GBS, an autoimmune disease that happens from a nerve paralysis virus, and it is rare. It only happens to three to four people among one lakh people."

"When did this happen? I have no idea about what it is, never heard about it," she was shocked but confused at the same time. Even though she didn't know what it was. The ratio of three in a lakh seemed to stick with her.

"Yet, again, not a lot of people know about it, but that experience was far worse than this. For a moment, I thought, it would become a permanent part of my life, and I will have to live with it. I don't know how I got this rare virus, but it probably happened when I was in Delhi for my athletic training."

"What exactly is GBS?"

"It is Guillain-Barre syndrome. Even I had no idea about it." Sumit didn't want to seem like a know-it-all. He knew so much about it because he had experienced it. He told her about that day when suddenly he felt so weak and couldn't walk. Fortunately, he was at home only, so he called his mother for help.

"I was in so much pain that I couldn't even stand on my own."

When Sumit's dad came home, they went to the doctor for a check-up, and the doctor suggested he should get tested. In the test result, they got to know that he had GBS.

"It is a rare neurological disorder in which the body's immune system mistakenly attacks part of its peripheral nervous system."

"Now, what is a peripheral nervous system?" to Shivangi, every word felt like a bird. It flew above her head. She kept interrupting and asking what the technical terms meant.

"It is actually the network of nerves located outside of the brain and spinal cord. It can cause permanent nerve damage, in some cases, even death. Don't be surprised now. Even I had no idea about it. All thanks to this disease that now I know about it," he added sarcastically.

Shivangi smiled sympathetically. She knew her friend didn't want sympathy, but she was very empathetic and felt too bad for him. He understood her situation, so he smiled in return and continued, "We went to a hospital in Gwalior. My family doctor asked me to get admitted immediately."

Sumit got admitted to one of the hospitals in Gwalior but being a rare disease, not every hospital or staff knew the treatment. So, they had to change hospitals as well. Finally, after they found a qualified hospital, his treatment had started. "First, they injected immunoglobulin into my body."

"What is that?" asked Shivangi.

"It is an antibody made by white blood cells. They are a critical part of the immune response," he said, and she nodded again.

"The next day, I was admitted to the ICU."

"ICU?" Shivangi was shocked.

"Yes, but it seems so much smaller to what I have gone through," he sighed and continued. "I was there for a few days. I couldn't move at all. It felt like I had no control over my body. It's such a weird feeling. Can you imagine? Something as simple as walking, standing, or sitting that we do subconsciously, was taking so much effort. Even then, it wasn't in my control."

Shivangi was dumbfounded, she tried picturing herself in his situation, and she felt a surge of fear. She can never imagine herself going through that, having no control over her body. Before her thoughts could make her sad, she tried concentrating on his words.

"Two nurses were appointed to help me. I felt so helpless at such a young age. I mean, I am an athlete dude, and I had to take help from others to do the daily activities," he said, and Shivangi could see the sadness in his eyes. How much ever he tried to forget those days, he couldn't. Even if the condition was temporary, the experience was a permanent part of his life now.

"But you know one thing I realised on that bed."

"Yes, what it is?" Shivangi asked him with a spark in her eyes.

"No amount of pain can match the level of boredom or loneliness. That's why we humans are social animals. We need a company to survive."

Shivangi was confused with his confession. When she asked him more about it, he said that he had to stay in the ICU for almost five days, and those were the worst days of his life. Firstly, he had to share the space with two other patients as there were no private beds in the ICU. There were no phones allowed or any other activity for the mind as he couldn't move his hands. He couldn't even read. As an athlete who always stays active, those days of total stillness were like a ride of hell.

"So, if you compare lockdown was better and fun for me," he added.

"Seriously, now I can understand Sumit. I am sorry for that." Shivangi didn't know what exactly she should be feeling. She felt awful for her friend, and on the other hand, she felt happy and grateful that she never had to go through any such thing in her life.

"Don't feel sad. That made me stronger to fight the viruses like these."

"Oh, yes. I agree," she said readily. Sumit sensed the tense moment, and he wasn't very well in these types of situations, especially with friends. That was the first reason he would never tell his friends about this, but he knew Shivangi was a very good friend. To lighten the mood, he added,

"So, the people I was sharing the ICU with, one of them was an old woman, and she expired while she was lying just beside me. Trust me, that lady haunted me a lot in my dreams."

"Really?" Shivangi had goosebumps.

"Not really. I was joking," he laughed, and she breathed a sigh of relief.

"Stupid, who jokes about such matters?"

"Relax, yes, she did die, and the incident was terrifying. I didn't lie about that. Only the dream part," Sumit said with a soft smile, and she replied with a silent, "Oh."

"Wow, you already went through these hospital miseries which people are experiencing in this pandemic."

Sumit laughed and quickly added, "This is just the beginning."

And she responded with another, "Oh."

"When they finally shifted me to a private ward. I was happy after a long time, at least there was some progress, and I needed to get out of the room."

"You were happy for being shifted to another room?" she asked and then realised that it was a happy moment for someone who had been through so much in five days.

"It was one of the happiest moments of my life. I have realised how and why a patient feels happy by these minor changes," he said, and Shivangi remembered how her sister Ruchika had talked about her father-in-law. He was so happy after being discharged.

Sumit felt a lot better after they shifted him to the private ward. His health was improving, and soon, he seemed fit and fine. So, the doctor discharged him. But after the first two weeks of returning home, the treatment relapsed. He had to be admitted again. But then his parents thought and decided that they would take him to Delhi for better treatment, as so many hospitals and treatments in Gwalior had not helped him. That was the second time his treatment had relapsed.

"You went to Delhi?"

"Yes," Sumit continued to tell her how, and when they reached Delhi, they didn't get an appointment for two days and had to wait in the hospital lobby. Then they finally met some experienced doctors.

"They injected an artificial plasma into me. My throat was badly infected that they had to put a tracheostomy into my throat."

Sumit saw Shivangi's confused face. And before she could ask, he explained, "Tracheostomy is an opening created at the front of the neck, so a tube can be inserted into the windpipe to help a patient breathe."

With every word, Shivangi's eyes widened a bit more, and her jaw dropped in shock.

"It was the most uncomfortable thing I have come across in my life," he said, and she gulped in response. Sumit's experience was getting more uncomfortable with every new detail.

"Fortunately, the treatment helped me, the result was good, I could stand, but I needed some support to walk, like a wall, a person or a stick."

"It's great that you were finally able to walk," Shivangi sighed in relief that finally, the deadly experience came to an end, but then he spoke again.

"Not so great, I then had to admit for the third time after around fifteen days. Then we finally went to Bhopal, but there I thought these people were experimenting on me as this disease was rare. No one had any idea. However, after a few days, a senior doctor came to the hospital, he put me on steroids. Then after one week, I was totally fine."

"Were you fully cured?" she asked. She didn't want more surprise elements in the story.

"Yes, but I had an attack again last year before the lockdown, and I was admitted immediately. Thankfully, I haven't had any attacks since then."

"Thank God, dude. I know, I can't feel what you went through, but I am so happy that you are finally better."

"Yes, me too, and of course, no one can understand what exactly I went through, except for the people who have had GBS," said Sumit and chuckled.

"I agree." she gave him a sympathetic look.

"So now you understand why Covid is nothing for me in comparison to this?" he asked with a soft smile.

"Yes. I can see that." she smiled back.

Shivangi had realised that there were things worse than Covid.

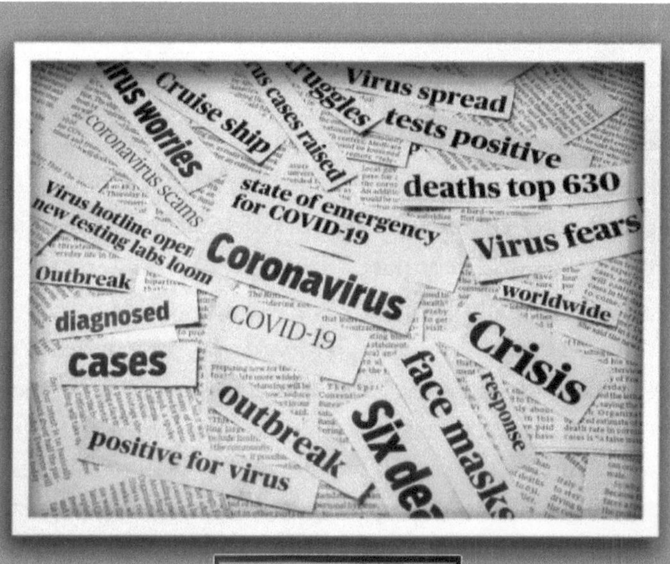
Virus spread
tests positive
deaths top 630
Cruise ship
Virus worries
Coronavirus Scams
state of emergency
for COVID-19
Virus fears
Virus hotline open
new testing labs loom
Coronavirus
Worldwide
Outbreak
diagnosed
COVID-19
'Crisis
cases
response
Outbreak
face masks
positive for virus
Six dea

COMING SOON

14

THE REPORTING

"*Di*, please call me when you are free."

Shivangi left a voice message on Nitya's WhatsApp while watching the news channel Nitya worked in. Nitya was Ronish's daughter, and she was a reporter.

It was mid-April, and things were worsening day by day. The second wave was storming strongly. Every day Shivangi would sit with her father and watch the news. She had stayed away from the news because of its negative impact. When the world was hit by the second wave, there wasn't a full lockdown, but only partial curfews and rules. So, she had to stay up to date with every new regulation. Shivangi and her dad were always worried about Nitya, as her job had a lot of risks, especially during this pandemic.

She wondered what the reporters could do, apart from working during the pandemic. Not only the doctors or the policemen but even the journalist were risking their lives and stepping out to provide us the information.

She thought about Nitya. She was living in Delhi, working as a journalist. Being a thirty-year-old woman, and living alone in a city like Delhi, has not been easy for Nitya. Mainly she was so busy during the pandemic that she wouldn't even pick up her calls, sometimes not even on Sundays. Nitya had to travel to different places to report their condition during the pandemic. It had gotten hard to stay on the job for not only reporters but most of the people. They would do anything to keep their jobs, and for the same reason, Nitya was risking her life.

"I am mentally exhausted, but I am not the only one. There are other people in the media houses too. Some video journalists are struggling to stay on their jobs, as they are the first victims of this pandemic. Nowadays, people shoot videos on their own, mostly from their homes. My friend Yashika has no other option but to leave and go back to her hometown. I cannot afford to do come back. I have become an independent girl after so much struggle. People in this industry are losing their jobs in this pandemic. I am thankful that I still have one, and I can't screw this up," Nitya had once said this to her father when he asked her to come back home as it was not safe. Shivangi got to know this when she would occasionally talk to Ronish. He would tell her what Nitya was going through.

***

After two days, on a Sunday afternoon, Shivangi finally got a call from Nitya.

"Hey, Shivangi, I saw your messages. Now I understand why you don't call me anymore. I was out at a hospital last night, and then I went to the office to report the information I had obtained. The schedule is too messed up. Anyways, how are you?" she sounded relaxed.

"I am glad you called me *Di*. I am fine, we all are worried about you, we keep watching the news, and every single time it reminds us of you. How have you been?"

"Honestly, I need a massage right away," she laughed. Nitya had learned to be jubilant as well as serious. She knew her job was a very important one. She had to be very effective with every piece of information. But she even understood that she had to be herself with her family or friends. She would try to make things lighter so it wouldn't get too serious for the other person.

"I wish I was there for you. How are you exactly doing, *Di*?"

Shivangi knew about Nitya and how she would hide certain things from her family to not stress them, but she needed someone to share everything with. Shivangi was more than happy to be that person, not only for Nitya but for all her friends and family.

"Well, I am doing okay. Finally, I am at home, working from home but still resting is not a priority for now. I will have to head out tomorrow again. We have a lot of things to cover."

"Yes, I know, but you should still try to take a mental break. Just take care of your mental health and keep taking breaks when required. Though, *Di*, above all, you are doing a job that you love and are passionate about."

Nitya understood how everyone was worried for her. She felt a little happy about it, but she cannot always sugar-coat the reality, "It's not always about the passion, Shivangi. A news station cannot shut down. We all need to work regularly. Imagine you need an update, and you switch on the TV, but all you see is a black screen. How would you feel?"

"Yes, you are right. But when you step out of the house during these times of pandemic. Aren't you scared?"

"Obviously, I am scared. Everyone is, but it's our job. Just like a doctor or a policeman. You know that media is the fourth pillar of democracy, so it's our fundamental duty to provide necessary information to the public."

Shivangi agreed but then expressed her worries about all the false news and rumours and how it spreads to the public faster than the authentic news, especially during the pandemic.

"The main thing is to filter the authentic information. The public cannot always figure out what is right and wrong. Sometimes, you cannot trust the medium you get the information from," Nitya said. The free sites that provide information are not accountable to anyone. When it comes to paid articles or media sources, the information could be right because they are accountable to people.

Nitya also added that the main reason the rumours reach the audience is the availability of online platforms, and people believe the information basing it on popularity rather than its authenticity.

"Anyways, let's not jump into that. Why don't you tell me what's going on with you?"

"Well, *Di*, my life is pretty normal. I am free from all the work stress as there are no tennis sessions or college either."

"Oh yes. I wish I could stay at home and relax like that."

"I feel bad for you. Even dad needs to rush to the Airport in between hours and look at me, chilling at home."

"Don't be silly. By staying at home, you are doing the best thing for yourself and everyone else, and you don't worry about me. It's when I see people relaxing at home. I feel a little envious," she laughed.

"Don't worry, once everything is over, you can party again."

"Yes, I sure will. But for now, all my days are very hectic. I don't even have time for calling our family members," Nitya said sadly, and Shivangi gave her an "I know" look.

"I have to wake up early in the morning, and you know I am not at all a morning person," Nitya said sheepishly, and Shivangi giggled.

"I know how much you hate mornings, but now even I sleep like a lazy bear and sometimes wake up late."

"Oh, where has the sportsperson in you gone?" Nitya asked, a bit shocked.

"No, just my sleep schedule is messed up. As you know, being quarantined has messed up my schedule."

"I see," Nitya nodded.

Nitya wished, but she couldn't relate to Shivangi. She had a very hectic schedule. She would wake up early in the morning, drink tea, get ready, and leave for the studio.

"I always keep my dresses ready the previous night. But the main issue is for the broadcast journalists. They don't have any other option as they have to shoot in front of the camera," Nitya said.

"But it is hectic only because of the pandemic. I remember when the pandemic had just started, I was in my office on a normal day, then a lot of Covid case updates started to come in. A week after that, the government had an upcoming mandatory lockdown. So, our news director rearranged the schedule to provide for social distancing and asked us, reporters, to begin writing scripts and editing from home. Again, the same happened this year after the arrival of the second wave."

The thing Nitya loved about her job was that she got to collect the information. Research about it, and she set up stories for the channel. Last year, Nitya had an option to work from home, but she still had to go during the lockdown for three days per week.

"I am regularly going this year. The broadcasting journalists need to go every day, no matter what. Sometimes, my manager calls me on nonworking days. Some days I am one woman crew, filming, writing, and editing all by myself."

"You film?"

"I mean, I shoot, and the anchor speaks. I had to work extra during these times, but things are better this year."

"So, don't you all get breaks?"

"Yes, we do, but we have shifts. Though, we cannot have a longer break. Last year there were no breaks as nothing was open, so we could not go out for snacks or lunch. But this time we go to this coffee shop every day during my break. It refreshes us."

Refreshing was a very small word. Last year Nitya and many other reporters had to workday and night; in the studio, in the fields, in the red zones, risking their lives with no security of life or even a job. They would have seen dead bodies during their journey as a reporter, but deaths in such a high number was a new experience for every person who hasn't lived for more than 100 years.

"You know people are losing their lives. Every time I make a report, I try hard not to cry. It hurts so much to see people losing their loved ones. After some time, I got so used to everything that it stopped bothering me for a while. And then it affected me mentally because it felt like my heart had become a stone, but the reality was that my mind had adapted to the environment. That was the worst phase for me," Nitya said, and Shivangi was taken aback by the revelation. She had never thought about it from this point of view.

"Is it like when we see and hear so much bad news that even if we feel sad, we also feel like it's an everyday thing, and it doesn't affect us so much?" Shivangi asked, and now Nitya was slightly taken aback by the comparison. It was true. Nitya nodded, but she then changed the topic.

"This pandemic has become such a part of our life. We have developed habits we would have never thought of. When I step out, I sanitise my hands immediately, I hold the doorknob with tissue paper, and I use my car key to press the button on the lift. I have become so cautious."

Shivangi eagerly nodded. She understood what Nitya meant.

Covid has displaced many reporters and rendered them jobless. They fired journalists without being given any proper reason. Some lost their jobs, and some lost their families. They reduced salaries for the employees who maintained to retain their jobs.

"They do not think about the public anymore. It is all about profit for these private firms. They do business even during the lockdown. You can see the newspaper covered with full-page jacket advertisements."

"Yes, the newspapers are filled with ads rather than the news."

One of Nitya's friends lost his wife. She had Covid and was hospitalised. He worked in a news firm that went into loss. He didn't receive his salary for three months. He didn't have any medical insurance to cover his expenses and no money to pay the bills. Nitya and a few friends tried helping him by paying for his bills. He even sought loans. He wanted to save his wife, but even after doing so much, he couldn't save her. He had gone into depression soon after. He even changed his career as it kept reminding him of his loss.

"See, journalists are the gatekeepers of our society. But these harsh realities of the news industry hit us where it hurts the most-our morale, but all these things are hidden from the public," Nitya said sadly.

"But you don't have to worry, *Di*. We have got your back. I am sure *Chachu* is there for you."

"It's not about that, Shivangi. I want to be independent. I can't rely on dad anymore."

"Yes, you are right. I am just saying that you are not alone. We as a family are there for you."

"I know that," said Nitya with a smile. "Not only me, Shivangi, the journalists all over the world are working hard and have to face the same situation, but I understand it's our duty. Also, I enjoy it because I am doing something I love," she added.

"I know, but for me, you are my inspiration. It must have been so tough, and I admire you. You are strong. Your job requires too much strength. We feel terrified by listening to the news, and you feel it this closely, and that takes courage! Your field requires a lot of hard work and discipline. I look up to you. I must say everyone in the family looks up to you," Shivangi said with so much admiration in her eyes, and Nitya could hear it in her voice. She felt so happy to have such a supportive family. She thought she would cry, but she composed herself and replied with a soft smile, "Thank you, Shivangi. It means so much to me. I feel so good after talking to you, but I need to go now. We will talk later."

"Fine, go. I know how busy you are," she teased.

"I am never busy for you, Shivangi," Nitya said cheekily, and they both laughed.

15

MEMORIES

It was a stormy afternoon in May. Shivangi was sitting by the window, reading a book, sipping piping hot coffee while watching the beautiful rainfall outside the window. The pandemic was widespread, and a cyclone was coming towards their state. It has been raining heavily since morning. After reading a few pages, she closed the book, kept it aside, took her cup of coffee, and stood at the doorframe.

One day this time will be gone, and soon only memories will be left behind. After all, when someone dies, their memory is the only thing they leave behind, she thought.

The winds were very cold, and she was shivering. She rubbed her palms on the warm coffee mug.

"*Laado* (darling), what are you doing there. You will catch a cold. Come inside."

Shivangi's grandma lovingly called her *laado*. Shivangi smiled and sat by her grandma, it was her nap time, but the thunder had awoken her. She kept her empty cup down on the table and hugged her grandma. In return, she just patted her head. At this moment, Shivangi was missing her grandpa, who had passed away when she was only two. She was very close to her grandma. For her, her *Dadi* was the epitome of love and hope. Her grandma has always been the strongest woman, and she looked up to her as an inspiration.

"*Dadi*, isn't it true that things end but memories last forever? One day, all these noises, the problems, the debris on this planet will end," Shivangi said as she put her head on her lap. "You know, all the matter in the universe was created in one big bang at a particular time in the remote past which is known as the 'Big bang theory.' Even the earth was created then," Shivangi said, fascinated.

"Oh, I didn't know that. But did you know? There is an almost fifty-year-old book predicting that the end of the world was to occur in 2020. Following this global catastrophe drawn by unlimited economic growth by the global superpowers."

"Wow, *Dadi*. How do you know about the book?" Shivangi looked up at her and asked, intrigued.

"I have known these facts for so long. As you know, I was always passionate about reading."

Her grandma was always very active. Even at the age of seventy-three, she reads the newspapers daily. She understands every perspective, so she can freely communicate with her grandchildren. Hence, Shivangi never had a problem sharing things with her, which she couldn't even share with her parents.

"It is a bestselling book called 'The limits of growth,'" said her grandma. It was published in 1972 when the world began to wake up to environmental damage. The authors of this book were the first to coin the terms "sustainability." They said that without it, civilization would begin to decline by the year 2020.

"Well, who knows if this is true? If we look around, we can agree that even if the world has gained wealth, it has lost in terms of health. I remember, when there were no mobile phones, there was a telegraph to send and receive messages. Your *dada* (grandfather) and I used to send each other letters through that. Then your father used it to send and receive important letters from his college."

"Those times were simple. I sometimes wish I was a 90s kid. I find those times fascinating, also sometimes I feel these technologies are important but also very distracting," Shivangi said.

Her grandma softly smiled. She told Shivangi how someone's habits and lifestyle depend on them, not on the times they are born in. Even though technology has become an integral part of life, every person can choose their way of living.

"You can read more books to get a break," her grandma added.

Shivangi understood clearly what her grandma meant. Though she was now living in these times, she didn't use technology for everything. Even then, she was up to date with everything happening around the world. Shivangi nodded, and then she remembered an article she had read about the same topic.

"Professor Dennis Meadows explained that the factor, which was causing progress in the seventies, would lead to catastrophe in the early part of the next century," she told her grandma about it.

"Don't you think all these started in the year 2020? If we analyse it, then we can come to this conclusion that 2020 was chosen as the year of downfall," as Shivangi said the words out loud, she felt an unknown fear in her heart. She felt like everything that was written was going to happen. She was in her twenties. She didn't want the world to end so soon. She had so much more to achieve, so many years to live. Her worries were visible on her face, and her lips turned into a tiny frown which her grandma noticed and asked, "What's wrong, *laado*?"

"*Dadi*, I am a little scared now. What if these predictions come true?"

"No, *laado*, if you're asking if this is the end? Then no, the world will not end this soon, although there will be a lot of problems, disasters which humankind will have to face."

Her grandma explained how no one can ever know how and when this world will end. The pandemic put a break on everything, yet people are not going to give up and stop living. They will continue growing but only at a slower pace. The virus started from one country, and while everyone expected it wouldn't reach their country, it did. One by one, it became an epidemic and then a pandemic. For some people, it might be just a lot of deaths, but for someone who has lost their family, there's sorrow, pain, and grief-filled in people's hearts. They have lost their whole world, and the meaning of life has disappeared somewhere.

In the sixties, economies were growing, the development in the economy sector started to take place. These authors were worried about people losing to hunger, pollution, and industrialization, the price paid for growth.

"There's an old saying, 'No gain without pain.' Now the time to pay for all our gain has finally arrived."

"So, after so much development, this world will end?" she asked in disappointment.

"No, *laado*, I didn't mean that. It's my opinion. Eventually, everything will end, but it doesn't mean it will all happen in a go. It might break down different parts of the world. It can be called our karma, but it's not right to conclude anything. These books are evidence that the destruction has already started to take place. For example, look at our country. Some parts are getting struck by a cyclone. Look outside; there's a storm," her grandma paused to breathe and then added. "There's a theory by Malthus, which suggests that, whenever there is overpopulation, nature takes a step forward to reduce it, and this is what is happening to our world."

"Have all good things faded away, *Dadi*? People are dying, and we can't do anything. What else is worse than helplessness?" Shivangi asked innocently.

"Good things never fade," her grandma resolved all her queries in a single sentence. It was true. However difficult the situation gets, there's always hope. The feeling of helplessness and guilt is the natural response of humans to the challenging tests of life, but the truth is, humans have evolved to survive. There's an utmost need to save oneself before offering a helping hand to others. Her grandma told her to be grateful for the sun that shines every day.

"Look closely at the world. People are helping each other to survive this deadly virus. The dedication of daily sweepers, delivery boys, the pharmaceutics, volunteers serving those patients selflessly and endlessly. From police and journalists to doctors, they are all blessings to humankind. They are selfless beings that give us hope. Meanwhile, all we can do in return is to pray for their safety," her grandma said and quickly added. "And follow their instructions during these difficult times."

Shivangi said nothing. She felt so blessed to have her grandma, who could soothe her worries in a few words. She smiled at her. Shivangi's admiration for her had increased double-fold as she smiled back. After they both sat there in silence for a while, her grandma picked up the remote from the table, switched on the television, and turned the channel to the news. Shivangi quickly grabbed the remote from her hand and switched off the television. When her grandma looked at her puzzled, Shivangi shook her head, saying, "No, *Dadi*, we are not going to watch the news. You will then start overthinking, and then it will affect your health."

Her grandma grabbed the remote back and sniggered.

"Are you talking about yourself? I don't overthink. That's your department. And how will I have these interesting conversations with you if I don't keep up with the news?" she said and switched the television back on. Shivangi was looking at her dumbfounded, jaw dropped. Her grandma put the remote below Shivangi's chin and closed her mouth, saying, "Now, shoo, go talk to your friends or your diary but don't disturb me. Go, go."

Her grandma shooed her, and she laughed. She stood up with her coffee mug, took her book, and sat by the window again, now looking at her astonishing grandma.

Well, who knows when and how it might happen? We all will die one day, and that's the ultimate truth. Memories are timeless treasures of the heart. No matter how much time is gone, memories remain in our hearts. Life will end one day, but our memories will live forever, she sat there thinking.

16

ACCEPTANCE

Can history repeat itself in less than one year? Shivangi asked herself. The second wave of coronavirus had already hit the country, and it was more disastrous than the last one. It was at its peak. People had started to revert to their old lives, but here it was again.

Shivangi was tired of this life now. Last year, it was all new, so her excitement was super high, but this year after everything had resumed, they still had to stay home all over again. She was thinking all this when she got a video call from Diuja. That was it, she thought. *This is going to be my life- calls, video calls, and texting,* she huffed. She picked the call hesitantly. She wasn't in a good mood. As soon as she answered, Diuja asked, "Are you busy?"

"Yes, I have a meeting with the queen of England," said Shivangi, more irritated. Diuja understood, and she said in all seriousness, "You are lying. I just had a chat with her. She says she won't talk to you because you are being mean to your friends."

Shivangi rolled her eyes but ended up laughing.

"Of course, I am not busy, Diu. What will I even do? No work, nothing to be excited about. I will die of boredom," she complained.

"No worries. Captain Diu to the rescue," Diuja replied as she impersonated superman's pose. Shivangi was relaxed now. Diuja continued, "You know, I am attending this workshop for psychology. I have an essay assignment, and as you are the writer of our group, I need your help."

"Oh wow. I would love to help," Shivangi said, filled with energy.

"It has to be about the ongoing situation, the topic can be anything, and it's a vast topic to cover. So, yesterday my dad was watching a video about Japan. Their lifestyle and how did they cope with this pandemic. I got this idea to write about the country, like how they dealt with it. I found it interesting. I decided to do a bit more research and saved a few articles too."

Diuja told Shivangi about all her research. From the food to their lifestyle. Shivangi nodded along. She had got to know a few things from Dr Heenal.

"They eat boiled food only, especially rice with more vegetables with miso (fermented soybean paste) as a soup in their everyday meal. They have an active lifestyle. They prefer walking or travelling by cycle instead of taking any transport. They exercise regularly, which is known as 'Radio Taiso' or radio calisthenics. It is a short exercise routine broadcast daily on Japan's national radio, streamed on YouTube, followed in parks and schools every day by all generations. They follow strict timing for their meals and consume no drinks during those times."

"I have heard that they have a long lifespan, and now I know the reason," said Shivangi.

"I agree, and here forget about the diet food. People can't even live without street food."

Diuja further talked about the Japanese having seen so many epidemics that they didn't get frustrated with the idea of masks. They even have the three C's — closed spaces, crowded spaces, and close-contact settings. Shivangi was surprised by the information. Diuja said that she would write down the Essay and send her so that Shivangi could make the changes.

"The world was not ready for the acceptance. Japan was the country least infected because they had accepted the situation way before it reached them. They prepared for it," Diuja concluded. It seemed to Shivangi that the Japanese were more spiritually open. They don't live in the desire to acquire materialistic things. She placed her confusion in front of Diuja.

"We dream about materialistic things in life, like a new car, a new house, a loving partner, money, fame and what not but do these desires fulfil us as a whole?"

She wondered if it is said, rightly, that money cannot buy happiness. Are there spiritually happy people? She had read an article about renunciation and understood that it is conceived wrongly by people. There is no need to leave behind the joys of life to be more spiritual.

"Renunciation is the central theme of all the religions, and yet, is misunderstood. Several people changed their lifestyles and adopted a form of external renunciation. There are outstanding examples of people who lived a luxurious life. They enjoyed the best that the world had to offer, rejoiced in fulfilling family life, and yet were men and women of renunciation.

So, happiness is in our mind, not in the object. Initially, the spiritual path seems like a punishment. You think you will lose everything you love and relish. It is like a child seeing his father's life as boring. All that dad does is work in the office the whole day. He does not engage in anything the child finds exciting.

Everything we strive to find in this world is in our minds. Mind is the one playing all games, whether it's the craving for lust and materialistic things or being on your own, discovering yourself. In this pandemic, people are bound to go on a journey of self-discovery."

—(Article Credits: Speaking Tree, The Times of India)

Shivangi read parts of the article that she found interesting. Diuja listened carefully.

"Simply put," Diuja started and paused to collect appropriate words, "Umm, our happiness is in our minds, not in the materialistic things we crave. Like my happiness lies in having more clothes. At the same time, someone else is happy in their daily routine."

Shivangi nodded. They both sat silent for a while. They were thinking about how life has come full circle. They both were at the same place as last year. Looking at the positive side yet craving the freedom of life again.

Shivangi was happy for the moment that she was safe. Her friends and families were safe but staying within the four walls had been tiring for her.

"It feels like I haven't seen the world since forever," she exasperated.

The virus was mutating, and the power of the infection was intensifying every day. And the world is divided into two groups. One group of people feared the virus even more than before, and the other group accepted the virus as a part of their life and moved on. They were no more surprised by the outcomes of this pandemic, focusing on hoping, praying, and being optimistic about the future rather than ranting it out like the previous year.

"No one knows when this will exactly end anyway," Shivangi sighed.

Her thoughts were spiralling into the world of illusions. She wondered if humans lived in an illusion of dreams and fantasies. Being amidst a pandemic, they still think and plan about when it's over. The things they would like to do. Like planning a vacation, going on a road trip, hanging out with friends, etc., to finally be able to move on the roads freely and what not. No one ever stopped thinking of the wishes and desires to be fulfilled post-pandemic.

Of course, it was the hope to recover from this destruction, but will all this come true? What if it doesn't? We never ask this question. We are profound to know when this will end, and we will finally be able to live in a Covid free world, Shivangi thought.

As if Diuja had read her mind, she said, "Our generation does live in a fantasy world but isn't that a powerful thing if used correctly."

She enhanced the idea that our mind pictures days when lives go back to normal like before the pandemic, and the mental desire to overcome the situation keeps the optimism alive through the pandemic.

"As the time passes, we are coming closer to the acceptance of this new life. We have acknowledged it with hope and kept moving on," said Diuja with a smile.

"But, bro, what if all this never ends? What if we would have to live in these circumstances always?"

No matter how much Shivangi tried to accept the changes, it always came back to her like a blow. The "What ifs" never left her mind. She remembered how, at the very start, when the news of the outbreak of this virus spread, everyone observed and hoped that it wouldn't reach their country.

"I remember, we were chilled out here like it won't reach us. We refused to believe the consequences because of our preconceived notion that it won't last long in our country, but soon, we realised that it is here and now we will have to face it," said Diuja.

"It took around two months of lockdown to realise that it is not going to be normal easily, and we will have to accept the situation," Shivangi added.

Diuja suddenly flashed a wide smile like she had cracked some high-security code. Shivangi's face conveyed nothing but pure confusion. Diuja showed her index finger to the screen as if asking for a minute and then ran to grab some book from her study table. As she sat back down, she turned page after page until she landed on that one page she was looking for. She read for a minute while Shivangi patiently waited. Diuja finally closed the book and looked up at Shivangi, "You know, I had taken psychology in my 12th class, and in college, I continued it. I studied about a theory on accepting things."

She explained to Shivangi how they could look at the situation and understand it with the help of the grief cycle.

"We have now psychologically accepted this change, and there is a philosophy called the 'Kubler Ross Model.' It is the grief cycle given by an American-Swiss psychiatrist Elisabeth Kubler Ross in 1969. When a human goes through any tragedy, natural disaster, or accident, they pass through five stages of grief. These are denial, anger, bargain, depression, and acceptance," Diuja said.

She had compared and merged the theory with the current situation. Starting with the first stage- denial. The denial phase was when people refused to accept that this virus could travel to their own country.

"And when it came, we repeatedly denied that it will not spread due to the hot climate conditions."

Shivangi was intrigued. Wow, she thought it was correct. The next stage Diuja explained was anger. Anger surged throughout the crowds as soon as the virus started impacting their life. Their response to the loss of income or the normal life was anger. Most of them got so consumed by their anger that they set out on the path of violence. Shivangi gave a quick nod.

"Coming to bargain, this is the stage that lasted the longest."

In the bargaining stage of grief, humans attempt to postpone the sadness by imagining "What if" scenarios. From the very start, our minds had started triggering these what-if situations. From "What if the virus doesn't reach us" to "What if the virus stays."

"Half of us are still in the bargaining stage," Shivangi said.

The next stage was depression. This year was the mark when mental health became quite a topic of discussion. People were depressed for so many reasons. From simply being isolated to losing everything in life. It was the suddenness of the situation. It is something no one has ever faced or even imagined. No one was spared, from the rich to the poor.

"Of course, bro. Mental health has been attacked badly. People with higher income felt isolated and lonely due to the lockdown. So, we can imagine what mental state had been of the people who are barely surviving," Shivangi replied.

"A lot of people are now finally acknowledging mental health, thanks to the lockdown. Now, finally comes the last stage, which is acceptance," Diuja continued.

The virus is a part of our lives, and subconsciously some people have already accepted that. They know that they will have to live with it.

"There are people who still haven't accepted the situation. They still deny the fact that it will remain with us for a longer time." Diuja said and added. "We have to accept and set the next steps to progress in life instead of living in the imagination that it won't affect our lifestyles."

"The irony is that even if we deny it outwardly, somewhere, we have absorbed it so deeply that it is not such a big deal. It's like, yes, the virus exists, but now what are we supposed to do? Live in fear, forever?" Shivangi said raising her eyebrows.

"But can you notice the way we have accepted had led us to a bigger apocalypse in the country? We started taking it casually, forgetting about the consequences," Diuja concluded.

We humans can accept and move on in our lives instead of being stuck in one place because life is shorter than we imagine it is. Acceptance is a part of human life in the context of psychology. Humans accept any situation, eventually.

I wish you
were not
here !

17

PANDEMIC CHILDHOOD

It was late June and the last Sunday of the month. Shivangi was extremely bored. It had been a few months since Ayaansh left for Delhi. He got his admission and was currently living with his aunt Jiya. But unfortunately, his classes were online. Shivangi spent her months occupied, but today she missed her younger brother.

She thought, how weird sibling bond is. When Ayaansh was here, they would spend every day fighting at least for half an hour, and now she was missing him so much. He would often call and talk to everyone at home. In the beginning, their conversation was limited to asking how they were. But soon, they both would sit and chat about what was going on at both places. He would tell her about his college, and Myra, their little cousin sister, and Shivangi would talk about her day. He often said he missed home as he was stuck there on the fourteenth floor. Although he had Myra to keep him entertained and attended his college lectures online, he badly missed home.

Shivangi usually called him on Sundays, as he was busy the rest of the week with his online classes. She dialled him, and the phone rang, but he didn't pick up. After a few minutes, she got a call back.

"Give me the phone, Myra," she heard from the other end. It was Ayaansh's voice.

"Hello, *Didi*. How are you?" asked Myra as she ran away from Ayaansh and hid behind her mom.

Before Shivangi could answer, she heard her aunt sternly say, "Myra, give back Bhaiya's phone."

Finally, Shivangi heard Ayaansh on the call.

"Hey, *Di*. Sorry, my phone was with Myra. First, she didn't pick up as she was playing, and then she won't give it to me."

"Hey, it's okay," she laughed.

Ayaansh and Shivangi talked as usual about everything and anything. After a while, she heard Myra asking for the phone, saying that she wanted to talk to her elder sister. When he finally handed Myra the phone, she started talking without stopping for a breath. Myra complained about her mom, Ayaansh, and her life. She said how he was always busy on the laptop, sometimes studying, sometimes playing, and he would never take her downstairs to play with her friends. Even her mom would not let her go out. Instead, she would often ask her to watch television.

"I want to go play with my friends, Samarth, Manan, and Yuvika. I want to go to the playground," Myra whined.

"No complaining, Myra. I told you there is a Covid monster outside. It will grab you. Ask your *Didi*," Shivangi heard her aunt say.

"Is Covid monster real, *Didi*?" Myra asked innocently. She would believe Shivangi more than her mother. According to Myra, Jiya hasn't allowed her to do anything for the past one year. She would only tell her to eat vegetables, which she didn't like, and wouldn't even let her meet her friends. Even Ayaansh would always support her mother. Shivangi chuckled at her innocent question but seriously answered, "Yes, Myra. There is a very big Covid monster, but don't worry, many superheroes are fighting with it, and soon it will go away."

Myra flashed a big smile, so big that Shivangi could hear her smile. She jubilantly said, "Okay." She passed the phone to her mother and ran to her room.

"Hello *beta*, how are you? How is everyone?"

"Everyone is fine, *Bua* (aunt). How are all of you?"

"We are okay, but I am worried for Myra."

When Shivangi asked her aunt about her worries, she said Myra missed travelling. Most of the days, she would sit and look outside the window. There was no school, no playtime in the park. She had not seen her school friends for months. She was becoming more and more annoyed and agitated. She would often keep pestering Ayaansh to play with her, even if only at home. But with time, she understood that he was busy. Even her father had work from home, and he couldn't spend much time with her during the lockdown.

"Myra is directly in the fourth standard now," said Jiya.

"Wow, this is great. Did she pass the online exams on her own?"

"Not exactly. Ayaansh helped her a lot."

"See, we don't know what will happen next. I had bought Myra's uniform in March, as we thought that the school would reopen, but nothing happened."

Shivangi said nothing. She didn't know what to say. She has never thought about the situation from this point of view. They were worried about their health, education, and career but had forgotten about how so many children's childhood was spent among four walls.

"We had an option for online or offline, but now again, everything is online. Another year will be gone, and soon I will know that she is in the fifth standard now," Jiya sniggered.

Jiya was worried about Myra's growth. Kids learn from the environment more than they learn from books. Now Myra was caged in this environment. How was she supposed to learn anything? Even though they had online classes, Jiya felt it was of no practical use.

"Sometimes she is so bored that she will help me with cleaning and stuff. Even though she can't do much, she tries her best. Whenever I feel she has done enough and I tell her to stop, she would say, 'you don't want me to play, study or help you clean, what am I supposed to do in the house the whole day?' Such a cute little munchkin she is," her aunt said, and both smiled at her innocence.

Shivangi thought about the term she came across so many times but never paid attention to 'pandemic baby.' Babies born and growing up during this pandemic were going to be so different. First, their immunity would be a little less. As Shivangi once learned, the more unpleasant environment a person lives in, the more immunity they have. These pandemic babies were born in times of sanitization. Their physical development was tough during these times. As Shivangi processed this thought, it worried her a lot as she was a sportsperson herself.

"*Bua*, don't they have an online P.E. class?" Shivangi asked, even though she knew it could sound stupid.

"No, they don't, but I worry about it too. At the start of the lockdown, she was very active, but now she has adjusted to this lazy lifestyle. She wakes up late and mostly spends her time on the phone and TV. Even I can't say anything about it. How will she ever be physically fit?"

"Doesn't her school conduct any activities?"

"She had to perform online on Zoom call during her function in school once, and you know those few days during rehearsals and performance, she was the happiest. It shows how physical activity is important for her happiness too. Now she misses her rehearsals and dance performances," said Jiya. "At such a young age, she has to see all these. During this time, she should be going out, playing, falling, hurting, learning, and now see what has happened. It feels like her whole childhood is being wasted."

Myra had adapted to the changes very well during the last year. She knew she had to wake up, watch Ayaansh setting up his laptop to attend his online classes and sometimes Myra's too, for her to attend an online class. Then she watches television or uses the phone, complains about not being able to go out, and then sleeps. The excitement of going to the school had almost vanished. She had accepted her life to be boring. The only happy moment in her day was when she would watch a Barbie movie or play video games with Ayaansh on the Xbox. It was her favourite part in the evening.

"The pandemic has at least taught them hygiene and importance of immunity," Shivangi said. Her aunt just hummed and then bid bye to Shivangi and passed the phone to Ayaansh again.

Shivangi and her family were going to shift to Delhi very soon. Ayaansh had taken with him most of his belongings, but a major part of his packing was still to be done, and rather than coming back, Shivangi was given the responsibility to pack the rest of Ayaansh's stuff. So, she planned she would pack on Sundays when she was on a call with him so she could ask him about anything related to packing his stuff. She sat in his room surrounded by his things and kept packing. While packing, she poured her heart to him about how she felt about Myra and her childhood. Not only Myra but so many children were never going to experience a real childhood. Even if it is only for a year, a child can learn so much in a year.

Ayaansh agreed with her. He was seeing first-hand how the pandemic was affecting Myra. He remembered something that had happened at Myra's school, and he felt like sharing it with his elder sister.

***

Myra was given a school assignment in the holidays, where she was supposed to write how she felt about the pandemic and lockdown. Ayaansh helped her with the project by suggesting what she could write, but she bluntly denied his help. But neither Jiya nor Ayaansh saw her work on it.

"Myra, did you complete the assignment?" enquired Ayaansh the day before submission.

"Yes, *Bhaiya*," she nodded.

Ayaansh let it go. The next day after Myra's classes, Jiya got a call from Myra's teacher about the assignment. Her teacher said that she wrote only one line.

It read, "I wish you were not here!"

***

Shivangi was stunned and speechless. Somewhere Shivangi agreed with Myra, and maybe everyone did. She had expressed her emotions in a few words. A little girl, in the fourth grade, always cheerful and jubilant, was so dismayed by the pandemic. When she expressed all her thoughts to Ayaansh, he said nothing more than, "Well, it is what it is- a Pandemic childhood."

18

THE FRUITS OF HIS DILIGENCE

Finally, by August, Shivangi's whole family had shifted to Delhi. Shivangi was excited yet sad to leave her childhood home. She had spent her entire childhood in that house. She felt something weird, like leaving a part of her life behind. It was a massive change for her. She could not believe what exactly was happening to her. In her lifetime, she had never shifted anywhere before. But it happened upon her graduation. They had completely shifted, but still, some amount of work was left.

"We need to get the floors ready as fast as possible," Amita said to one of the laborers.

To which he gave a reason which she ignored. They have been waiting for so long. The work had started months ago, and still, when they completely shifted, they had to keep things packed in boxes so that they wouldn't collect dust.

"You people have to work faster. It has been three months. How much more time will it take to refurbish the floor?" She asked.

"Just a few days more, madam. We had to do other works too, and it takes at least two days to dry," said one of the laborers.

"What other works?" Amita questioned. She was very frustrated.

"Madam, we had to reconstruct the walls, the kitchen, and room and even do the painting. So, it will take a little more time," he explained.

"Okay, take your time, but complete as fast as you can," she agreed. She knew they were not wrong.

***

Due to work going on, everyone had to sleep in one single room. It was Sunday, and Shivangi was yet to wake up. She had planned that she would sleep till late. All the packing and moving had tired her. But she was awoken by the drilling noises, and hence she woke up irritated. She walked to the hall where her whole family, except Ayaansh, was sitting. He was still sleeping, and Shivangi was amazed at how he could sleep in such a noisy environment. The first thing she did was walk over to her mother and complain about the noise. She missed the peacefulness of her old house. Everything was messy, even the air. "Mom, it smells really bad here. When will this construction end?"

"It will take some time, *beta*," Amita consoled.

In the hustle-bustle, the morning passed quickly. It was afternoon when Amita gave tea to the laborers before they left for their homes. As it was a Sunday, they would work half-day only. When all of them sat and had tea, Sanjay, who was seated on the couch in the hall, asked one of the laborers, "How much will you exactly charge for refurbishing the floor?"

"Sir, it will cost around forty thousand for refurbishing the hall."

"That is too expensive. You need to lower the cost."

"Sir, we are asking a reasonable price."

The laborers felt that they had been working hard for the last three months, and the cost they were asking was quite reasonable as they had to refurbish some parts of the hall. Sanjay, however, disagreed with their point. He felt it was too much. Amita tried to convince him, saying that it was a decent price for the hall and the room, but then, he confirmed that they were charging that price only for some parts of the hall.

"This is too much. You have to reduce the charge. Otherwise, I will contact another contractor for the rest of the job," Sanjay reprimanded, but instead of being afraid, one of them stood up to him and told him that he could do that if he wished, but they wouldn't reduce their prices.

"These laborers are charging too high. I don't understand how they are so confident," Sanjay whispered to Amita.

Amita shrugged. Both were confused with the laborers' confidence. Then one of the laborers stood up in frustration and told them that they were charging nominally based on the number of square feet. If Sanjay wanted to enquire with another contractor, he could, but he would not find cheaper rates. Sanjay didn't like the tone of the labourer, but his point was right. He had contacted many contractors, and these people were the best and more reasonable.

"Fine, but you need to work faster," Sanjay ended the conversation with this.

Before he could get up and leave the hall, one of the other laborers spoke, "We will, sir. Otherwise, how will we feed our families? We are hungry for work. I remember not working in the lockdown. Give us a chance. We will complete with good work." Sanjay heard him and calmed down a bit. He knew he had overreacted, but the air had filled with frustration.

"Okay, I am trusting you, but the work should be good. Only then we will pay the full amount," he said, and the labourer nodded in agreement.

***

The next morning, the laborers were back at sharp 9 am. When Amita asked them if they would have breakfast, they declined, saying they had it at their respective homes. They needed to complete the work. Their concentration was only on working. Soon, the day turned into noon when the laborers went for their lunch break and then came back to work. Around 5 pm, they all took a tea break. Amita served tea and biscuits to all of them.

All of them were conversing among themselves. Shivangi was standing beside her mother having her usual cup of coffee when she heard one of them saying,

"Rajesh *sahib* (sir) was saying he will pay us half of what we have asked. But then how will we send money at home? Why are these *sahibs* not understanding? We have got work only after lockdown. We are surviving on this income."

Before Shivangi could interrupt, Amita had already raised her question.

"I saw the news about you people. About all the laborers leaving the city and going back to the village. Why were you all in a hurry when the government promised they would do something?"

"No one will do anything for people like us, madam. Those were mere promises. We had no earnings. Every construction site had been closed. We had no option but to go back to our villages. At least, we have our own home there. We won't die hungry there." The guy who had convinced Sanjay about the cost said. Shivangi remembered his name was Raju.

"Oh, but didn't you have your savings?"

"These savings don't last long in these big cities. We are poor people. We have to feed our children," added the one who had answered that day about the price. His name was Murali.

"Weren't you afraid of traveling in groups? Without any social distancing."

"There is nothing like this virus. This is just a game by the state. It is an illusion," said another labourer, but the others shushed him. Shivangi then thought about the people who still believed that this was a rich person's game to ruin the poor.

Raju came forward and kept his empty teacup on the tiny table beside the couch. He went back to his place and told Amita about their experience.

They had travelled thousands of kilometres on cycle when the nation was in total lockdown. He had to travel from Delhi to his village in Uttar Pradesh. Along with him were many other laborers traveling to the same destination and some traveling to their villages in other states.

"There was a curfew. We were jobless, hungry, and dependent on the government. So, we all decided to move."

Amita asked in shock how they covered all this distance on cycle. Another one of the laborers came forward to tell them about his experience where he had to walk as they did not have a cycle or any other transport.

"I had to gather five thousand rupees from all my savings so I could travel back to my village," said Raju.

One by one, all the laborers started pouring their hearts out to Amita. No one had asked them this, and here madam was listening very calmly.

"Madam, even the food given by the state was not good. The best option was to go back to our houses," said one of them.

"It was the worst. I had to take my wife and kids to the village without any footwear to wear," added another.

During the lockdown, there was no work in these cities. Rather than begging, they sought a better way was to go back to their homes safely. They further added that they got no help from people in the city. Neither did the government do anything in the beginning. Sometimes the police would beat them up if they went out to the shops, too.

Amita was taken aback by the immense response. She didn't know all this, even though they had kept watching the news. Now she felt like the news didn't narrate the whole truth.

"Seems like you people were forced to leave without any transportation. But the thing is, everyone was scared. It was mandatory to close the trains and the buses," she said softly.

But the laborers were now tired of the excuses. They had to endure so much that they have stopped accepting these excuses. They felt like they were the only ones who had to suffer so terribly while people with money stayed safe at their houses.

They remembered they had to cross the Ganga River because they weren't allowed to go by road. They had to cross the river in a boat as the locals would not lend them the ferry in fear of being beaten by the police.

"Oh my God, this is bad. Though these were the state rules, still they could have understood," Amita gasped.

"No one understands us. This is the truth," said Murali.

They continued telling them about their travel. As they were travelling by cycle and even barefoot at times, it took them six-seven extra days. They had adapted to the reality and let it go, but then came the issue of food.

"We even asked for food from a Minister of legislature assembly, but he didn't even look upon us."

"How did you ask?" asked Shivangi. Until now, she stood there silent, but this intrigued her.

"We contacted someone. He said he would arrange food for us from the community head's office. He was a volunteer, he sent the list there, but we didn't get any ration."

"So, how did you eat then?" she asked.

"People would come from *Gurudwara* sometimes, and they gave us food, that too not every day. Once in a few days, we were able to get dome food, that too only one meal, it would be two chapatis and a bit of vegetable."

Amita nodded in understanding while Shivangi had her next question ready, "How did you know the directions?"

Raju answered this question as well. It seemed like he was the leader of the group. He said that one of the members would use their phone and guide all the others through google maps. That person would keep the phone in one hand and ride the cycle with one hand only. Both Amita and Shivangi were surprised first by their experience and then by the fact that they had smartphones and the internet.

But we live in the twenty-first century. It is not a big deal, she thought.

When Amita said they had suffered too, most of the laborers sniggered.

"Madam, leave it. We know how it was for us. We had no other option rather than travelling. I have been working in Delhi for nine months. I have four children- two boys and two girls. They were in our village, and they had been calling me for so long. I thought I would go back home during the harvest season, but then the lockdown happened. We initially thought it would be for one day, and we could endure, but then it kept extending. We again tried adjusting, but how long was I supposed to stay?" Murali said promptly.

Amita nodded, not knowing what to say.

"How will we survive if it keeps extending? No one thinks about that. What will a poor person do? Only people like us can understand what we went through. During our travel, we asked the people from the villages we crossed. They helped and guided us. No rich or powerful came to our rescue. We are the only ones protecting ourselves," he said with pride.

Amita and Shivangi looked at each other and then sighed. They knew that they couldn't do anything but listening to the stories of these laborers made them sad. Everyone fell silent, and only sighs were heard. Then one of the youngest laborers of the group spoke. He had kept quiet all the while. His voice was barely audible, his figure was lean, and he looked like a malnourished child.

"I am just twenty-two, living with my parents. My sister is married. I need to provide money to them. My wife lives in our village, and I miss her a lot, but I don't have any other option apart from surviving this somehow."

As he finished, the room fell silent again. Breaking the silence, Amita softly asked, "Now, do you all have work?"

"Yes, since there is no lockdown, we have work. But we don't know till when because these rich can cause trouble in our bread butter by giving an excuse of this disease," replied Murali again.

Amita nodded again and stood up to collect all the cups. She went to the kitchen, wondering how different her life was from theirs. She knew that the fruits of his diligence had to be sweet.

The last labourer's words reminded Shivangi of one of the stories about a worker that she had read in an article. It was sort of an interview.

"I am a migrant worker from Jharkhand. A week into the lockdown, my employers in Delhi refused to give me any salary. They didn't even pay me for February. I am the sole bread earner of my family. I need to take care of five others. What am I supposed to do now? I used to earn twenty thousand a month, and now I don't have any savings.

In April, I stayed at a place provided by our employer with twenty others. How could we possibly maintain social distancing? Then, our employers announced that they would pay us only if we were willing to deliver the food and supplies to the nearby hospital. I had already heard a lot about the hospital. I knew I might get contaminated with the virus. I still went there and was scared. I didn't want to take the risk. I have two young kids. Who will take care of them if I die? I begged him to let me stay until I could figure out a way to get back home, but he disagreed.

Then I registered a complaint to a nearby police station, and luckily, I got a response from them. They had to agree and pay for my tickets, but nobody followed any proper hygiene guidelines. We weren't even given a sanitiser . It takes around twenty-one hours from Delhi to my village Barkagaon in Jharkhand. I had to change bus every few hours because there was no direct bus. It was a nightmare for me. It took me more than twenty- four hours to reach my village. I was pushed around to shift buses, and there was no social distancing. Everybody was tense and was only discussing this virus. We were all worried about our family's safety and health. I met a man who lost his father due to the virus. Another one, who didn't know where his children were. I came across a lot of people who were going through major changes due to this pandemic. The troubles faced by them were unbearable.

Compared to them, my situation was better. I didn't want to think about the future. I was just grateful that I was finally going back home. After reaching my village, I was quarantined. I couldn't go home for around twenty days. They kept me in the isolation ward in the nearby town's Hazaribagh's medical hospital, which was a town nearer to our village. There was no isolation ward or a bigger hospital in our village.

I was there for around two weeks. Then it was extended to six more days. The days were tough. Even after I was home, I couldn't meet my family. I used to pray every day to God for my well-being and that I didn't start showing any symptoms.

When I reached home, the other villagers were petrified of me and didn't talk to my family properly. I have lived in Delhi for over twelve years now but was forced to leave the job, and I had no savings. Now I am in my 30s and will have to start my life all over again. I have seen with my own eyes how terrible it is for thousands of us. Our only fault is that we are poor with no choice. I hear some people are complaining about not being able to go out. While here, I am wondering about how I will feed my family. How will we survive?"

Shivangi remembered the story, and once again, it left her eyes damp. She slightly brushed off a few tears from her eyes. She got up and went to her room, all the while thinking, *there are still a lot of* unheard stories, which might make us emotional, but we can't exactly feel what they went through.

19

BLESSINGS IN DISGUISE?

"Hi!" both Shivangi and Diuja screamed as they took each other in a bear hug.

"Oh my god. Finally, we meet," Diuja said and again took Shivangi into a hug.

It was October, and she had come to stay at Shivangi's place for a few days. It was also Shivangi's birthday week. After all the phone and video calls they had over the last year and a half, along with the previous year when they both couldn't meet because of living in different cities, they finally met. Both couldn't contain their happiness. As soon as Diuja placed her luggage in Shivangi's room, they both sat down and talked and talked until their throat went dry. They even missed lunch and directly left the room at dinner time.

It seemed like they hadn't talked for a lifetime. Their talks were never-ending. It was 2 am, and they were wrapped in blankets, sitting on Shivangi's bed, and gossiping.

"So, what are we doing for the next few days?" Diuja asked. She knew Shivangi would have already made a full-proof plan of what they were going to do.

"I haven't planned anything. I thought we would do whatever you want."

Saying Diuja was shocked was an understatement. Shivangi loved planning out things, and here she was without a plan. Diuja understood that the year had changed people, maybe in a good way.

She asked Shivangi to take a paper, and they both sat and wrote whatever they wanted to do in the span of the next few days while Diuja listed her wishes.

The next morning, both woke up around 11 am. First, Shivangi looked at her clock and then took her to-do list, which they made the night before, and put a tick in the first box. It said wake up after 11 am. No wonder they both loved sleeping.

Even though they had planned what they were going to do, they ignored the chit of paper and randomly explored the city and fulfilled all the desires they were holding down in their heart.

They tried many new dishes, hung out at cafes and restaurants, and drove around the city. They shopped so much that Ayaansh almost asked if they both were planning to open a dress shop. They even spent hours doing photoshoots. It was like they had enough photos for the next few months, but overall, they loved spending every minute with each other.

On Shivangi's birthday, they spent the whole day doing the same stuff they love doing. Shivangi was so happy that finally, after the last pandemic birthday, she could go out and celebrate. She got so many calls and messages from all the people she knew. Half of her day went in answering calls and responding to birthday messages. When they cut the cake, she received calls from other people too.

***

It has been a week since Diuja has been with Shivangi. She had to leave the day after tomorrow on a Sunday. Diuja told Shivangi that she had planned to go and chill at a cafe for the next day. When Ayaansh heard this, he commented, "Chill? At a cafe? Then what were you guys doing all these days?" to which Shivangi and he ended up fighting again.

The next morning, Shivangi was ready for the day, but she felt like Diuja was busy with her phone since morning and even the previous day. Diuja didn't look as excited to go out either, which in turn ruined Shivangi's excitement too, but she let it go as her friend was leaving the next day. She wanted to keep up her spirit.

The drive to the cafe was dull too. Diuja was still on her phone, as she was getting a lot of calls. Shivangi was getting frustrated by the minute. Yet again, she didn't say anything.

It was a red signal. Shivangi was impatiently tapping her fingers on the steering wheel. She looked beside her at the passenger seat, where Diuja was sitting. Suddenly she was reminded of an incident that had left her shaken for a while. Everything around her resembled the setting of that day.

***

I was in the driver's seat, driving my friend back home. All the while, she kept talking about her father. Stories about how she travelled with her father. When we stopped at the petrol pump, she fished out her phone and showed me a picture of her father. Why? I was thoroughly confused but didn't let it show. Maybe she is really close to her father, the same way I am.

It was a red signal when I heard her say that. I was numb and shocked. My hands were shaking. I knew I had to drive through it. The steering was in my hands, but it felt like I had no control over them. My mind had gone blank for a while. I somehow drove and accidentally bumped into a car in front of me. Thankfully, the cars had just touched, and nothing happened, but the news had created a mess in my mind.

She told me that her father died last year due to Covid. All this time, I thought that she just loved him so much that she kept narrating his stories. But the moment I realised that it was the pain speaking, my breath hitched. She said that it felt like he was still here.

He was in the hospital when he had Covid. A few days later, she got the unfortunate news.

"My dad didn't have any bad habits. Neither did he drink nor smoke. He didn't do anything which might have harmed him, but he couldn't survive."

I didn't know what to say. I didn't know how to console or comfort her. As she got out of my car, I just gave her a warm hug and bid her goodbye. I continued driving throughout, my mind filled with chaos. When I reached home, I slowly walked to my room and wept. Without a single word uttered, my eyes kept spilling.

***

The constant honking and Diuja's voice brought her back to the present. She shook and nodded her head at Diuja's questions because she wasn't really listening. She had forgotten how that small incident left her with such deep emotions. Clearing her thoughts, she concentrated on driving. Meanwhile, counting her blessings.

They reached the cafe, found a decent table, and sat down. They were chilling and talking before the barista came to get their order.

"Yes, I am so happy. We are finally living this time. Patience is the key, though I miss Shrant a lot," Diuja said sadly, but somewhere Shivangi felt that she was faking sadness.

"Don't be sad. You met me after years, but it did happen, right? So, you will get your chance to meet him too," she consoled her anyway.

"Also, I have been eagerly waiting for my college to reopen, and they are giving us assignments. I mean, look at these colleges, there is a global pandemic going on, and they are more worried about these assignments. I mean, what's wrong with them?" Diuja complained.

Shivangi just chuckled. As the barista got to their table, Diuja got a call, and she said she had to take it. Shivangi shrugged. As Diuja left, Shivangi scanned the menu and ordered coffee for herself. She knew Diuja would order once she returns.

She then looked around the cafe. She hadn't been out for so long. Even though she and Diuja were having fun the past days, there wasn't a day when she sat down and observed the world as she did during the whole lockdown. She looked around, observing people, things, and the environment. There were a few people who were so conscious that they had a sanitiser on their table, and some were so careless that she heard a guy say that he threw all his masks away and used the handkerchief as a mask in front of the police.

This is getting interesting, she thought, as she listened to people around. She was listening to many different conversations.

One of the teenagers was telling her friend how she learned so many new skills during the lockdown, and even though she wasn't a part of their conversation, Shivangi nodded and remembered all that she had done, like writing, learning Spanish, and even baking.

On the very next table was a man, who looked in his fifties, sitting alone having coffee. He was intently looking at his phone. As the tables were closer, when she looked carefully, she saw that the old man was looking at a photo of a guy who looked around twenty. She then saw the man rub his eye. It occurred to her that he was crying. That could be his son, who he lost in the pandemic.

She looked across both the tables again and understood how the pandemic had changed lives. Her eyes fell on the footpath through the window. She saw a young girl carrying balloons, trying to sell them. On the other end, she was enjoying the freedom that she got back, but that girl, even after the pandemic, was still trapped in the cage of poverty.

Till then, her coffee arrived, and the barista asked if she was okay because she looked a little dull. She nodded and said it was nothing. She thanked her and looked around again. She saw a few couples but among them was a table where a man was sitting with an older woman. It seemed like she was her mother. Shivangi couldn't hear what they were saying, but by their gestures and smiles, she understood that the man was grateful for his mother, and he was here to spend some time with her. Shivangi felt overwhelmed, but before she could tear up, suddenly the room erupted in cheers, and everyone looked at the table in the far-left corner. There was a family of five- father, mother, two daughters, and a son. It seemed like they were celebrating something. Shivangi didn't need to pay much attention because the daughter spoke loud and clear.

"Cheers to Mum for restarting her education," The middle daughter said, and the eldest added, a little quietly, "And to you for your UPSC exams." They all cheered once again.

"Wow," Shivangi thought, but she accidentally said it out loud. The family heard it, and they beamed a smile at her, and she smiled back.

Almost everyone was affected in some way or another. The intensity of it might be different, but everyone has lost something and gained something at the same time, she thought.

She had observed enough, and yet Diuja wasn't back. She was getting upset with every second.

To divert herself from all her thoughts, she started using her phone. She was sad that even when she was with her friend, she was passing the time like this. But then she heard someone clearing their throat as she looked up, and that second, her world stopped. She felt as if she was in a movie, and the crowd around her was a blur. She could only focus on that person. It was Varun! He coughed to get her attention, then forwarded his hands for a handshake, "Hey, I am Varun, and you are?" And within a second, Shivangi stood up and pulled him into a hug. He was surprised but happy and returned her hug.

They sat down. Shivangi had completed her coffee, and she didn't even realise it. Sip by sip as she watched people, she had finished her coffee. So, Varun placed an order for him.

"So, before you throw twenty questions at me. I will tell you what is happening."

Shivangi nodded. She was just about to ask him that.

Varun went on to tell her that he and Diuja had planned this date as he had missed Shivangi's birthday, so he wanted to surprise her. Shivangi felt happy, and now she understood why Diuja was on her phone so much. He then said that he had decided to stay in India.

"Wow," Shivangi shouted, delighted, but when he smirked, she calmed down and smartly changed her question, "How? I mean, why?"

"I feel lonely without my family. My mother doesn't want me to go either. I have found my passion here in the family business. I don't even have my job in Australia. So, I figured I would stay," he said and paused for a second before adding. "Even you are here."

As Shivangi heard those words, she felt like butterflies were dancing in her stomach. She gulped and averted her eyes. She asked that if he was an Australian citizen, how he would stay here. Varun replied that he would soon apply for Overseas Indian citizenship and would have a life-long visa in India.

"I see," she said, trying to hide how overwhelmed she was after listening to this. "So, the pandemic made you take this decision, right?" she asked happily.

"Well, kind of yes. I am happy here, doing what I love and with the people I adore," he said the last part, again, looking at her. She was confused about his words but let them go.

They talked for a little more time while he finished his coffee. When they were done, Varun stood up and told Shivangi that he wanted to show her something. She nodded. They kept talking as they walked across the cafe where there were rooms for celebrations. She looked puzzled, but then he asked her to go in. She stepped in, and her puzzled look turned into a cluster of emotions. She was shocked, happy, emotional, and everything in one.

"SURPRISE!"

There was a roar of cheer. There stood all her friends. Samaira, Swastik, Ricky, Prithvi, Sumit, Pisha, Shrant, and at the far-left corner was Diuja. Shivangi didn't know when she had started tearing up. Only when Samaira and Diuja ran to her and wiped her tears did she realise. Shivangi smiled brightly at everyone and hugged them one by one. She shook hands with Swastik, Shrant, and Prithvi as she didn't know them that well. They were here to celebrate her birthday. Belated birthday.

Ricky had baked a cake for her, and they all sang a birthday song and celebrated with joy. Shivangi was the happiest she had been in years. After everyone got their pieces of cake, she went by everyone to talk, one on one. She first went to Samaira and Swastik. She was so happy that she hugged Samaira again.

"So finally, a break from work?" Shivangi asked, and Swastik nodded before adding. "Had to do it for my darling here." he looked at Samaira but then winked at Shivangi. And they both ended up laughing as Samaira stood there and blushed.

"You know, now my passion, to become a doctor, has increased double-fold. After this pandemic and everything that happened. I have found real meaning in the field that I have chosen," said Samaira after a while.

Shivangi felt happy for her friend. She thanked Dr Swastik for everything he did for the nation amidst the pandemic. As Swastik went to chat with others, Shivangi giggled at Samaira.

"So, is this the dress?" she asked, and Samaira blushed and nodded. Swastik and Samaira would go on dates once in two months. Swastik would come from Hyderabad to Pune to meet her. Recently he had gifted her a beautiful black dress which she told Shivangi about but had forgotten to send her a picture. So, finally, Shivangi saw it now, and she knew this was it. Right then, Sumit came with Pisha. "We are here too," he said to get their attention and then introduced Pisha and Shivangi.

"You don't have to introduce us. We know each other," Pisha facepalmed.

Shivangi got to know that Sumit was back to his academy, now training young athletes.

"You know my students are so passionate about training. They don't want to skip any sessions post the lockdown."

"That's great. Well, you are a passionate coach too," Shivangi said.

Sumit developed gratitude towards life. Even though he had been through the worst of times which was even worse than Covid, he was still grateful that his family and friends were safe and that he had this life. Shivangi excused herself and went to get a piece of cake for herself, and as she tasted it, she felt it was so delicious and mouth-watering. She went to thank Ricky for coming and baking an amazing cake for her.

Ricky was doing better on Instagram and her business. She then introduced Shivangi to Prithvi. After talking to him, Shivangi understood why Ricky fell for him, he was the one for her, and Shivangi was happy for her. The one thing Shivangi loved about Ricky was that her mindset had changed with time. The way she changed from Instagram obsessed person to an independent owner of a bakery. She was having a fun chat with them when Diuja interrupted them.

"Okay, you met everyone. Now it's my turn for attention. I planned all this. You should thank me too," she said playfully. She wasn't expecting even a thank you, but Shivangi was thankful to her, so she hugged her and said thank you, which surprised Diuja. Diuja immediately turned to Ricky and teasingly asked, "What was in the cake?" Which made the whole room burst into laughter.

"So, you were being fake sad before. Because there is your lover, standing right there," Shivangi said, as she pointed to the corner, where Shrant was talking to Varun and Swastik.

Diuja just chuckled. Everyone was having the time of their lives. They talked about their blessings and how the pandemic was useful to them. Meanwhile, there were people craving to survive this pandemic somehow.

There is no doubt how the pandemic has changed people's career choices and lives altogether. For some, it has been a disaster, and for some, it has been a blessing in disguise, Shivangi thought.

SAN FRANCISCO
INTERNATIONAL AIRPORT
ARRIVALS
CHECK

20

A MASKED LIFE?

"Man had become far too reckless in his pursuit of materialism and this pandemic is like being nudged out of his reverie. If we understood its importance, it would seem like a second lease of life which is given to awaken man's mind and compel him to re-think about his life's priorities because in rethinking lies the secret of learning and discovering new ideas. This pandemic, therefore, is a blessing in disguise which will help man re-plan, course-correct and build a positive approach to life.

It is time now to acknowledge the blessings of our Creator, to undertake re-planning and re-evaluation of our lives, to seek contentment in what we have and not what we can have. Such an approach is the prerequisite to a healthy mind and will determine how one leads a positive, fulfilling and a spiritually nourished life."

—(Article Credits: The Times of India)

Shivangi knew that every word was true. She was, as usual, reading articles and had stumbled upon this one. It reminded her of the week following her birthday.

It was a cold winter evening. Shivangi sat with her diary beside the window in the hall.

"Dear diary," she started. Everyone else was in their rooms.

"It's the 30th of December. Can you believe the year is finally coming to an end? Let me tell you what a crazy year this has been."

She filled the diary with all her emotions. Her diary had the record of what happened for the past two years, from the first Covid case to the peak and the lows.

"One of the drastic things which happened this year is that I got admission for my master's degree. Well, as I was afraid, my online classes have started. I am sad that I might not get to enjoy my college life," she wrote in a mixed tone of excitement and sadness.

The danger of the second wave had passed too. Things have started to go back to normal. Shivangi's diary has witnessed her life change a lot. It has helped her to understand and adapt to the changes.

Still, there was an uncertainty in her heart. She did want things to go back to normal, but at the same time, she had formed her comfort zone in these times. Even though she hated being within the four walls of her home, that same thing had taught her so many life lessons. She learned about the world and herself. She connected with old friends and even found love. Well, not exactly love, but at least "More than like."

"Oh yes, I even forgot to tell you about Varun," Shivangi scribbled fast in her book.

***

A few days before Christmas, Shivangi and Varun were casually talking on the phone. It has become their daily routine now. Shivangi felt he was being very suspicious that day. He would say something, which she wouldn't understand, and when she would ask him what he meant, he answered with "Nothing." The worst answer ever. Finally, when Shivangi warned him that she would not talk to him if he didn't stop being creepy, he had confessed his feeling for her in one go. Shivangi was stunned for a moment, so silent that Varun felt she had cut the call. When he called out her name thrice, she came out of her trance, and without saying anything, she hung up.

Varun thought she got upset, but she had cut the call, only to call her two closest friends, Samaira and Diuja, to ask them what she should reply. On the one hand, Diuja scolded her for cutting his call and leaving him confused, and Samaira kept giving her a dialogue that she could use. When after a waste of five minutes she got nothing useful, she cut the call and ringed Varun. He picked up in a microsecond.

"I am sorry. Forget I said anything and never again cut the call without saying bye," he said in a go.

Shivangi was feeling shy and embarrassed at the same time. After mustering some courage, she confessed too and then as if karma was doing its work. She heard pin drop silence, but before she could call out for Varun, she heard a tiny, feeble "Yes!" filled with happiness. They both decided that they didn't want to be in a relationship just yet. But whenever they meet next, it would be their first official date.

***

"So, now you will have to listen a little less about my life as I have someone else, too, to share it with," she wrote and then turned to the next page and continued. "The last two months have been so crazy that I almost forgot to tell you about Diwali."

***

November 2021

The morning was filled with chaos. Shivangi's family was planning a grand Diwali celebration. Ronish and his family, including Nitya, had come to stay for the festival. Even Jigar, his wife, and Sakash had come and were staying at Jiya's place. It was a family reunion after so long. Shivangi was feeling elated. Just a few days ago, she had met all her friends, and now it was a family gathering. She finally felt like it was 2019 again with no hint of the virus.

"Things are back to normal," Ronish said. He and Sanjay were setting up the lights in the hall.

Ronish told his big brother about people going back to being careless regarding the virus. Only one thing that seemed to change was that everyone had a mask on. Some wore it like an eyepatch, and some like an earring, but carrying a mask was a part of this new life.

"You know it is like people have forgotten if there was anything like Covid at all. Only when they see other people with masks, they remember all about the deadly virus," Nitya added to the conversation. She had just come back from a long run with Shivangi, Ayaansh following them all sad and huffing. He didn't like to go for a run, but Ronish had told him to go along, and he couldn't say no.

As 2021 was coming to an end, the spread of the virus had reduced, things started to look normal. Some colleges had reopened, and some were still closed.

Ayaansh's college was still closed. He still had to attend his online classes. He had seen his campus only once when he had gone for admissions.

"All the classrooms are locked. The campus is quiet, and I don't know if I will be able to enjoy my college life ever," he had said sadly.

But now, seeing all the changes, he hoped that he would soon be able to enjoy the college life that everyone dreams of. Shivangi was waiting for her admission to start for the master's course. She hoped that she would not have to complete her master's degree online.

Nitya freshened up pretty soon, which amused Shivangi, but then remembered how Nitya had to manage her routine during the pandemic. It probably has become her habit to be fast. Shivangi chose to sit on the couch in the hall where Ayaansh was sprawled like a dead body, still huffing.

"That's why I say you should start exercising regularly, see you are still huffing," Shivangi sniggered. Ayaansh glared at her but said nothing because he knew everyone would support her.

Nitya made coffee for herself and sat on the sofa chair beside the couch. Nitya was back to her normal routine. It didn't feel new to her, but the good thing was, she didn't have to miss any party or gathering. Nitya had tested positive for Covid in June this year, and it was a very difficult time for her. When she recovered, she was so delighted to be free of the cage of her house and back to her busy lifestyle. And now, she was happier as her busy schedule was not so busy.

"My journalism days are on a break. I am working but at the same time enjoying life as well. The workload has declined after the lockdown," Nitya said when Shivangi asked her about it.

"I am glad that you came. I thought you wouldn't come, and I was so upset," Shivangi said.

When they were planning for the celebration, they called Ronish and asked him to call Nitya. But he said that Nitya was busy and wouldn't come. Shivangi was very upset, but then she decided to take the matter into her own hands.

"You said you are never busy for me, then please come," she had left the same audio message around ten times, which finally convinced Nitya to come.

"You know about my commitments. Now, I am here. We will have all the fun," Nitya said.

They were all gossiping when the front door opened, and both the ladies of the house came back from visiting Jiya. They had gone to meet Jigar's wife and see if Jiya needed some help.

The celebration was going to be in the evening, and it was at Shivangi's house. Jiya would bring the sweets as they would have Diwali pooja.

Once the ladies were back home, the chaos was back too. They ordered everyone to get back to work. They had a lot to complete in a few hours. The ladies started making the food for the evening, and Ronish made some *laddoos.* He knew nothing else in cooking, but his *laddoos* were the best. Ayaansh and Sanjay were putting up lights and flowers while Nitya and Shivangi made rangolis.

It was soon time to get ready, and one by one, everyone went to get dressed. Every once in a while, Amita would hear, "Where is my *kurta*?" Or "Where is my *jhumka*?" from her son and daughter, respectively. But before Jiya and everyone else had to arrive, everyone was ready at Shivangi's house.

"*Didi!*" they heard Myra's voice and saw her running through the door directly into Shivangi's arms. Finally, she knew that Myra loved her the most. Now there was hustle-bustle as everyone exchanged greetings and talked about their lives, catching up with each other. Shivangi was talking to Jiya. She said she was a little relaxed about Myra's school now as the school was planning to open by December. Shivangi nodded, being happy in her aunt's happiness.

She was going around greeting everyone when she started to hear one word more than she had heard Covid, "US" Sakash was at it again. *Boasting about the great country he lived in. Everyone was going to be irritated soon,* Shivangi thought. Gratefully one member of the family was brave enough to stop him. Myra looked at her uncle and sternly said in her cute voice, "*Mamu* (uncle), if you say, 'US' one more time, you will not get sweets." Sakash was stunned yet amused. He silently nodded, and everyone burst off laughing.

After the *pooja* and eating loads of delicious sweets, everyone was seated for dinner. Jigar kept telling how everyone should not take this break lightly as Covid might come back. He told them he regretted being careless, and now he was very strict about following rules. He was still telling everyone his "Ghost in the body" stories.

While everyone laughed it off, paying no heed to his words. Covid cases have almost reduced to three-digit numbers in cities. Half of India's population was already vaccinated. *Finally, things are back to normal. There is no way this virus will come back,* Shivangi thought.

***

Present

Shivangi didn't know that her words from that day would turn out to be false.

On November 24, the new variant of the Covid virus named "Omicron" was first reported in South Africa. Soon, in less than three weeks, it was all over the world.

Shivangi's last conversation with Riya and Tamanna was when they were leaving for the US after their stay in India.

"I have to go before another lockdown happens. I can't stay here for the next year also," Tamanna had said, and somewhere Riya had said the same.

Slowly and steadily, things were changing. People were adapting to these changes in their lives by taking baby steps every day. Ever since this virus arrived, people have started thinking more clearly. Their goals and priorities are clear. They look after things which used to bemuse them earlier.

A few days ago, it seemed like the pandemic had slowed down. Things seemed to get back. Then suddenly, the world is filled with the chaos of a new variant, stronger than before. Even though masks have become an integral part of everyone's life, almost like its mobile phone for today's generation.

Shivangi thought about how everyone's mind is filled with the same questions again. Some are asking, "Will there be a lockdown?" Some asked, "Is this more deadly than the previous one?" or "Is this the new normal?" But one question and the most important of them all is, "Will this masked life stay forever?"

ACKNOWLEDGEMENTS

I extend my deepest gratitude to my parents for supporting me in writing this book. It wouldn't have been possible if they weren't here to encourage me into doing something I am passionate about.

I would forever be grateful to my friend and artist Arjita Dangwal for supporting me in my ups and downs during the writing of my book. I thank her for making the illustrations for the book. That required a lot of patience and hard work. Furthermore, I would like to thank my friend Zeba Khan who helped me in coming up with the book title and a few other friends from Jamia Milia Islamia, who supported me in this journey.

I am thankful to my editor Dikshita Jain who understood my vision, worked on it with so much passion, and made my book more beautiful. I am glad to have found a friend in her. Thank you, Dikshita, for making my book extra special.

An enormous thanks to Inkfeathers Publishing for being such an author-friendly publishing house. For providing me with this opportunity to expand my horizon. I appreciate them giving me a platform to showcase my creativity and publishing my first book.

A very big thank you to you, the readers. I owe my success to you. Without your support, I can't fulfil my dream of transitioning from a writer to an author. This book is very special to me. Being my first solo book, I have put my heart into it. I hope you enjoy reading it as much as I enjoyed writing it.

Weirdly enough, you wouldn't be holding this book if it weren't for the deadly virus that entered our lives as the uninvited guest. This book was written in and about the pandemic. The lockdown had helped me become an author. In a way, pushed me to pursue writing.

INKFEATHERS PUBLISHING

India's Most Author Friendly Publishing House

Stay updated about the latest books, anthologies, events, exclusive offers, contests, product giveaways and other things that we do to support authors.

 Inkfeathers Publishing

 @InkfeathersPublishing

 @_Inkfeathers

 @Inkfeathers

 Inkfeathers.com

We'd love to connect with you!